TIPPY and the NIGHT PARADE

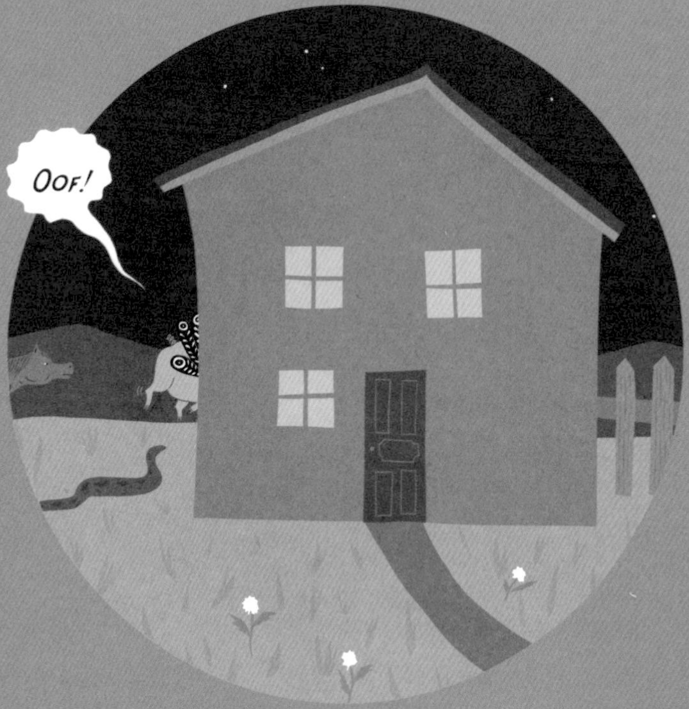
OOF!

Lilli Carré

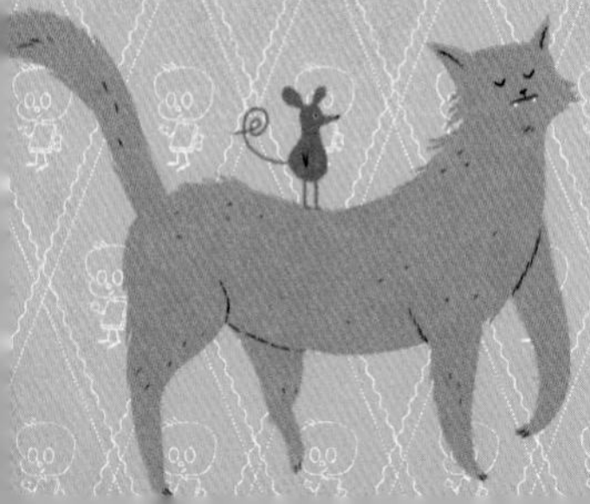

TIPPY and the NIGHT PARADE

A TOON BOOK BY

Lilli Carré

TOON BOOKS IS AN IMPRINT OF CANDLEWICK PRESS

For Alexander

Editorial Director: FRANÇOISE MOULY

Book Design: FRANÇOISE MOULY

LILLI CARRÉ'S artwork was drawn and colored digitally.

A TOON Book™ © 2014 RAW Junior, LLC, 27 Greene Street, New York, NY 10013. TOON Books is an imprint of Candlewick Press, 99 Dover Street, Somerville, MA 02144. No part of this book may be used or reproduced in any manner whatsoever without written permission except in the case of brief quotations embodied in critical articles and reviews. TOON Books®, LITTLE LIT® and TOON into Reading™ are trademarks of RAW Junior, LLC. All rights reserved. First edition: February 2014. Printed in Johor Bahru, Malaysia. Library of Congress Cataloging-in-Publication Data: Carré, Lilli. Tippy and the night parade : a TOON book / by Lilli Carré. pages cm. (Easy-to-read comics. Level 1) ISBN 978-1-935179-57-3 (hardback) – ISBN 1-935179-57-8 1. Graphic novels. [1. Graphic novels. 2. Bedtime–Fiction. 3. Animals–Fiction.] I. Title PZ7.7.C368Ti 2014   741.5'973–dc23

ISBN 13: 978-1-935179-57-3   ISBN 10: 1-935179-57-8

13 14 15 16 17 18 TWP 10 9 8 7 6 5 4 3 2 1

WWW.TOON-BOOKS.com

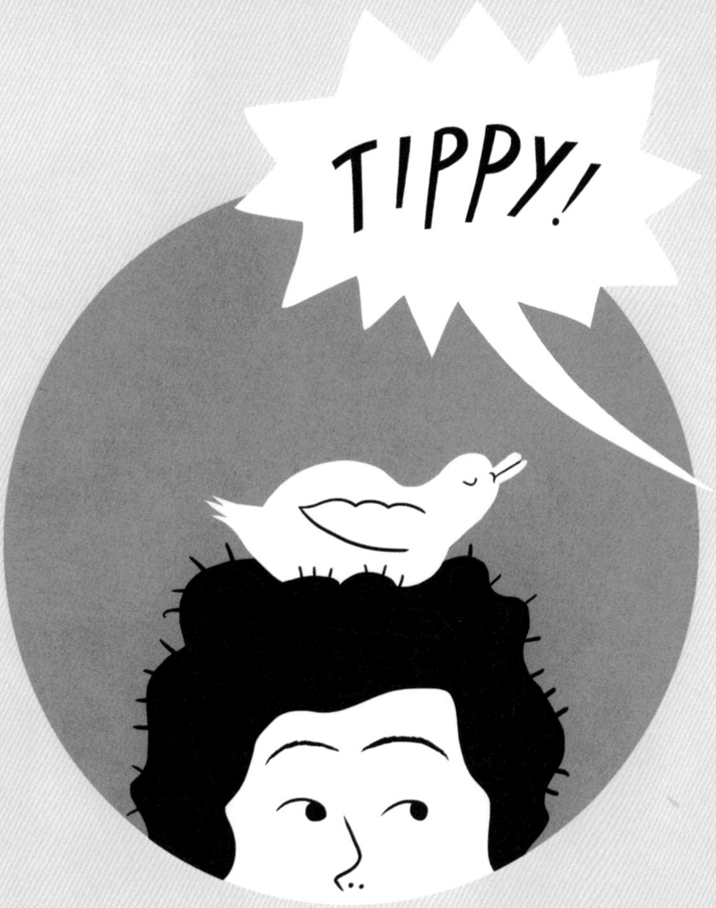
TIPPY!

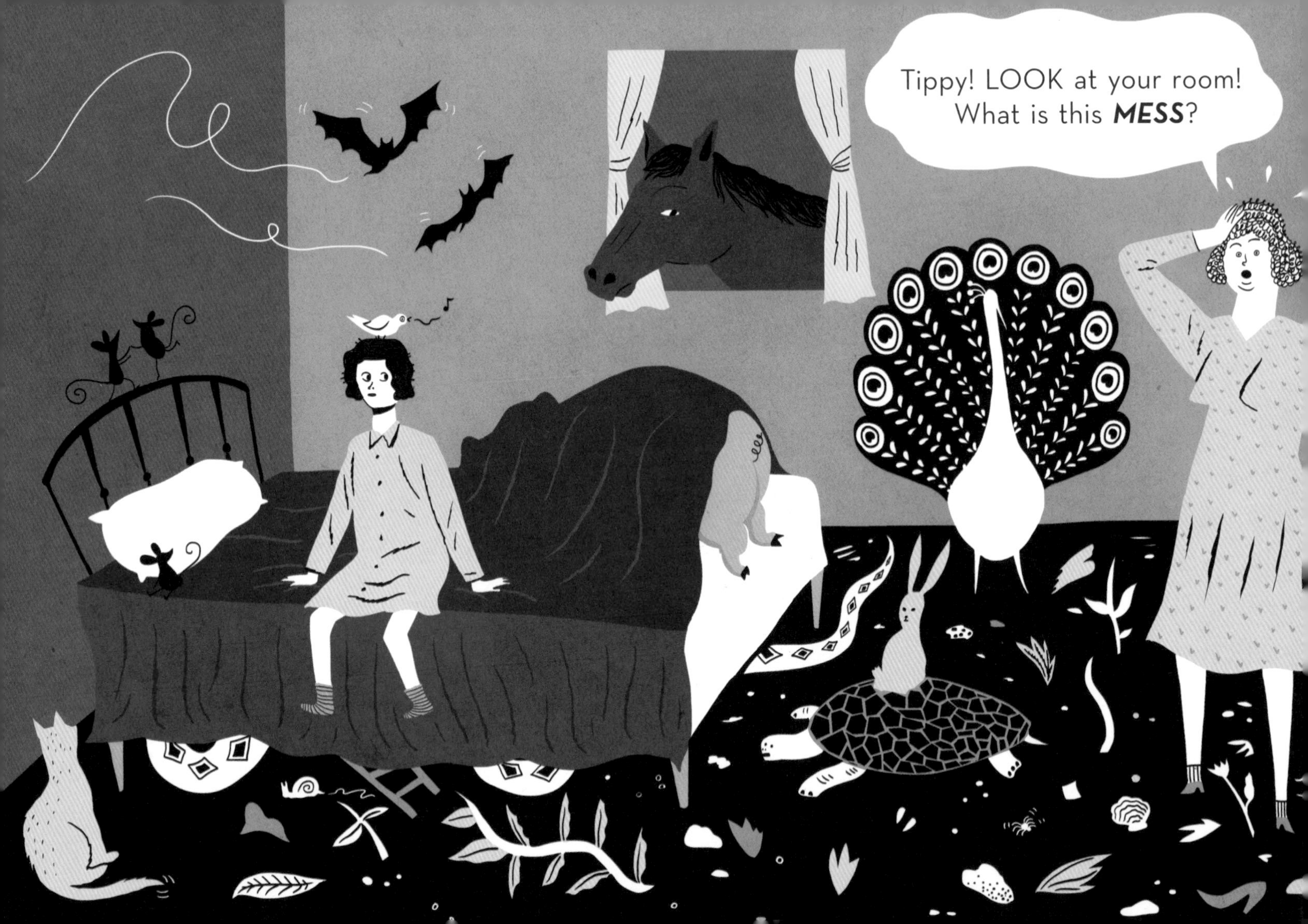
Tippy! LOOK at your room! What is this **MESS**?

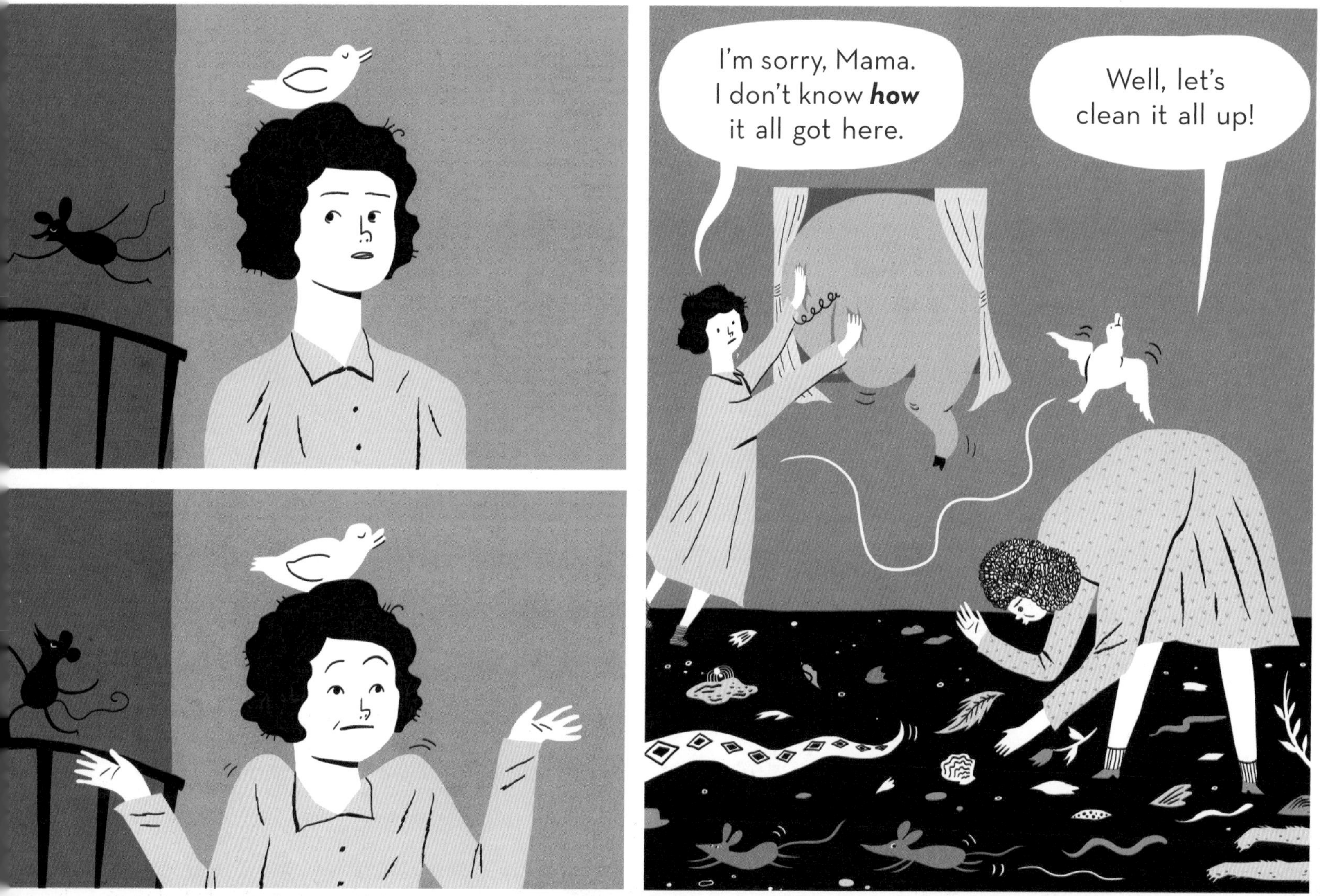
I'm sorry, Mama. I don't know ***how*** it all got here.
Well, let's clean it all up!

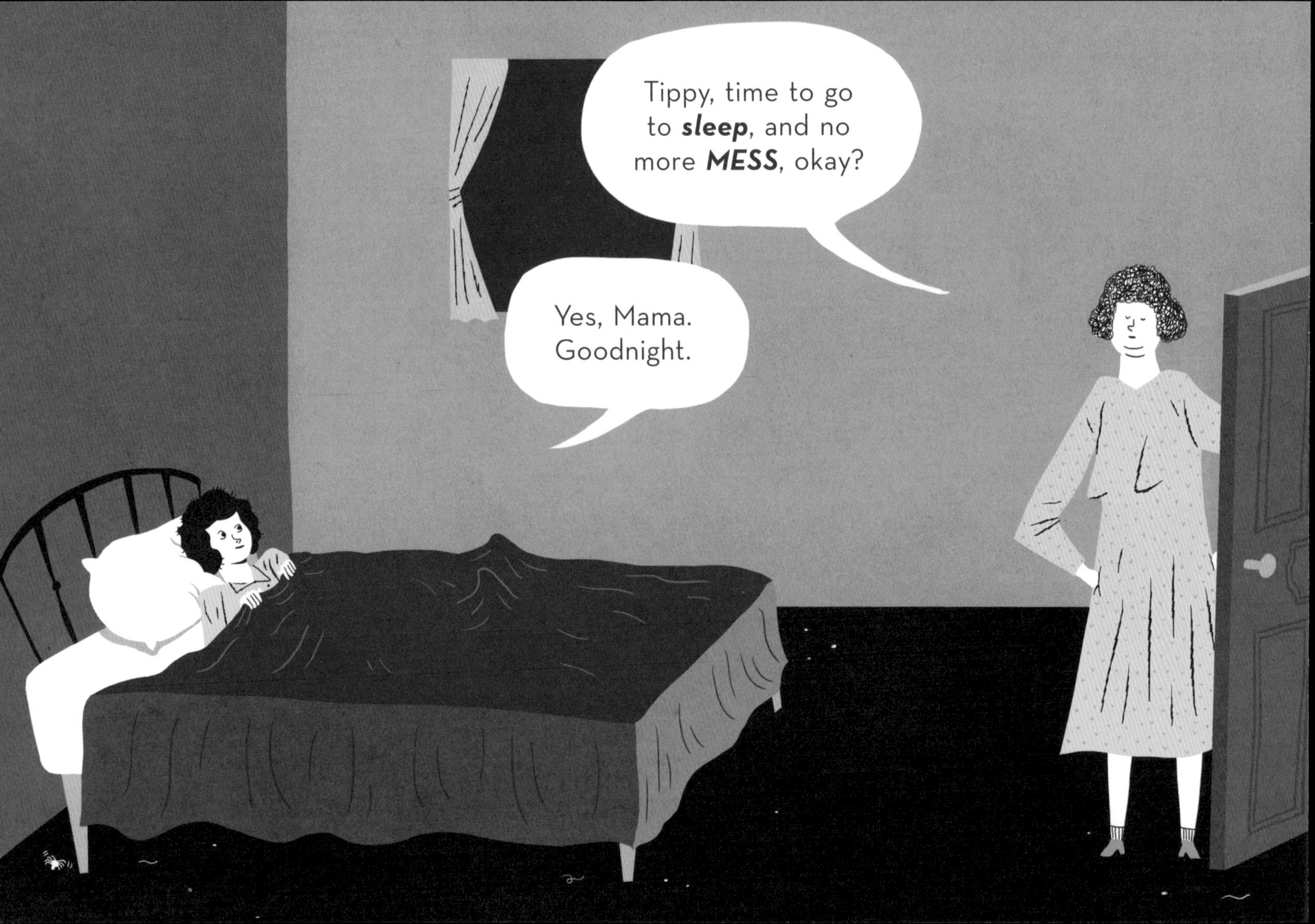
Tippy, time to go to **sleep**, and no more **MESS**, okay?
Yes, Mama. Goodnight.

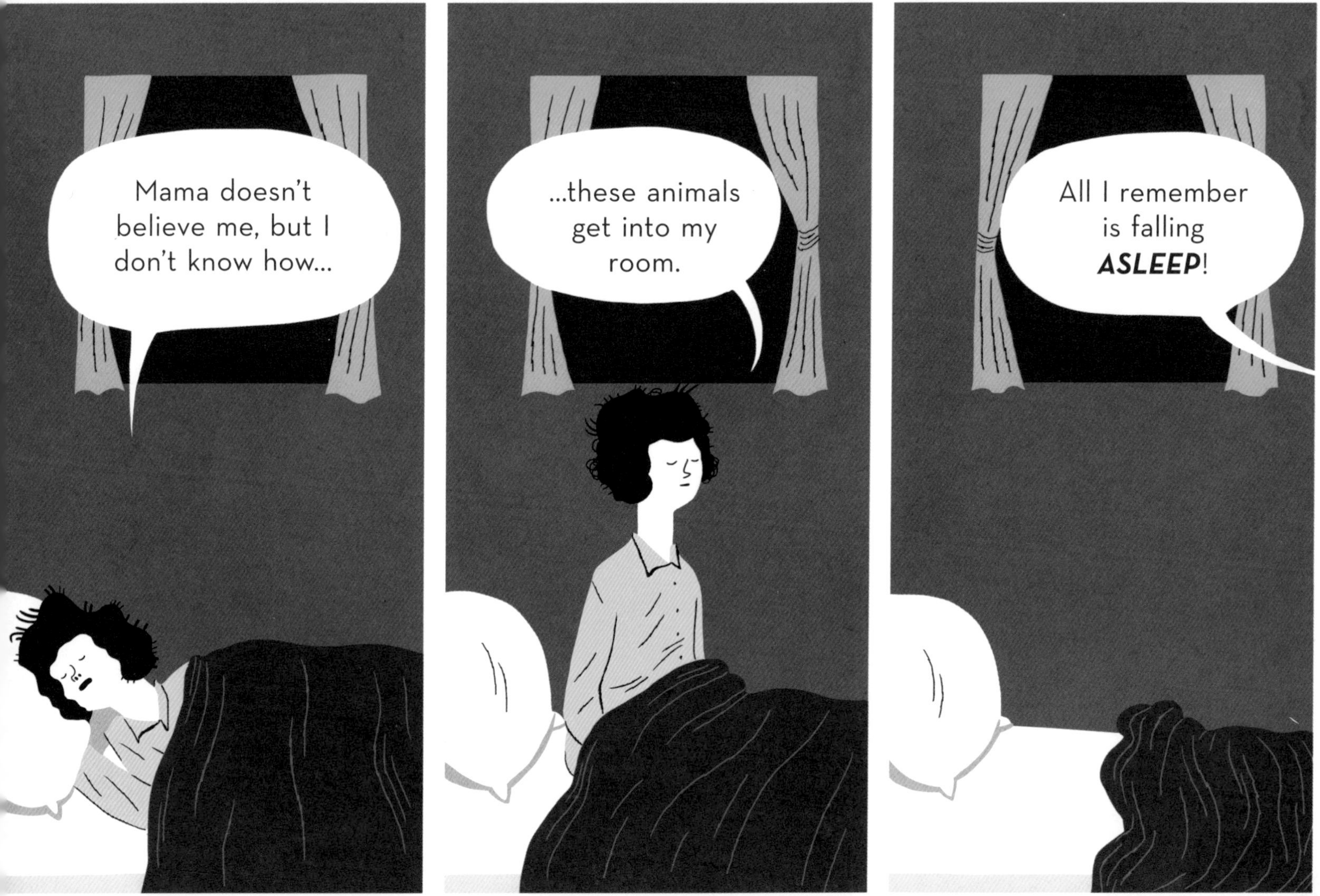
Mama doesn't believe me, but I don't know how...
...these animals get into my room.
All I remember is falling **ASLEEP**!

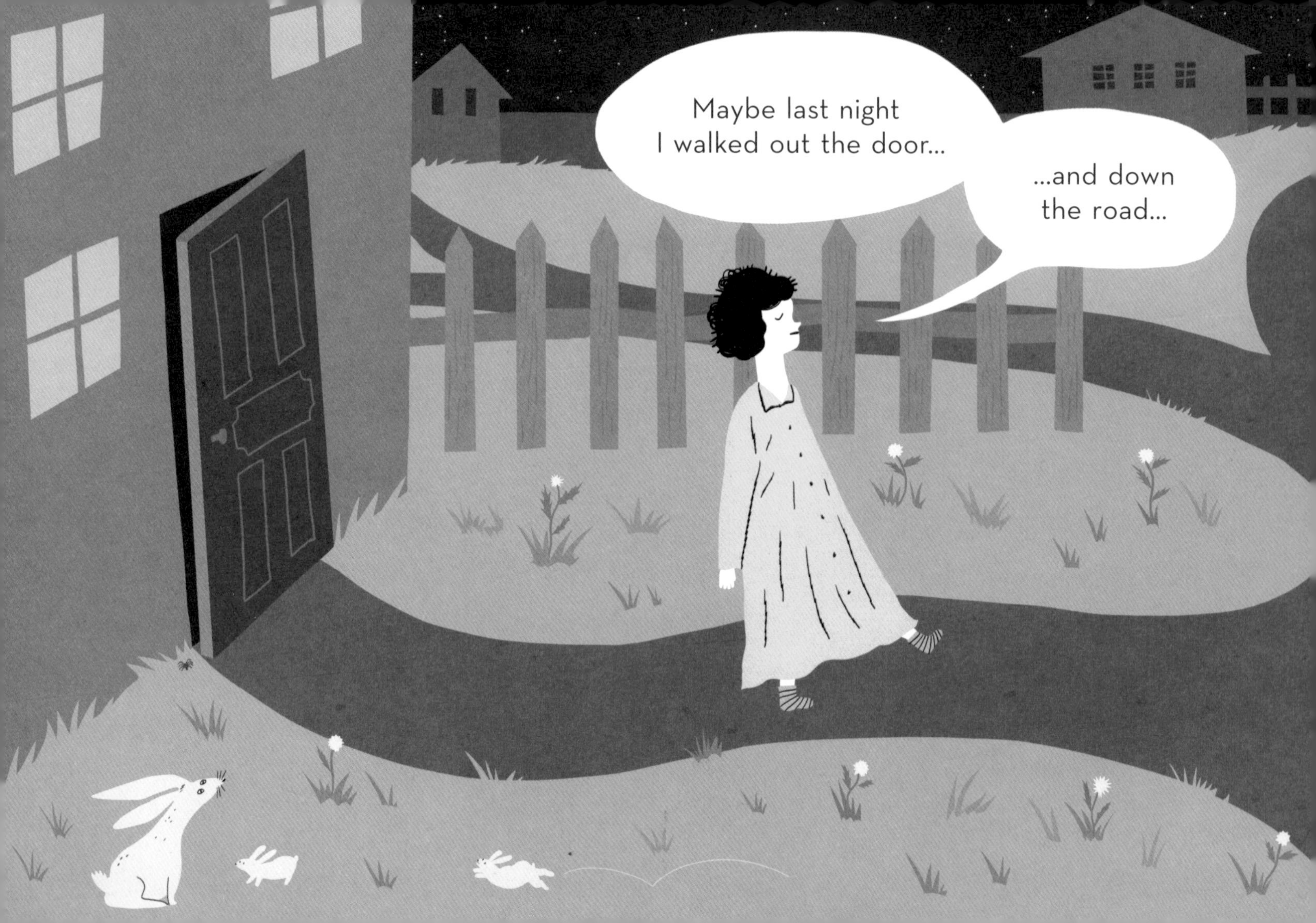
Maybe last night
I walked out the door...
...and down
the road...

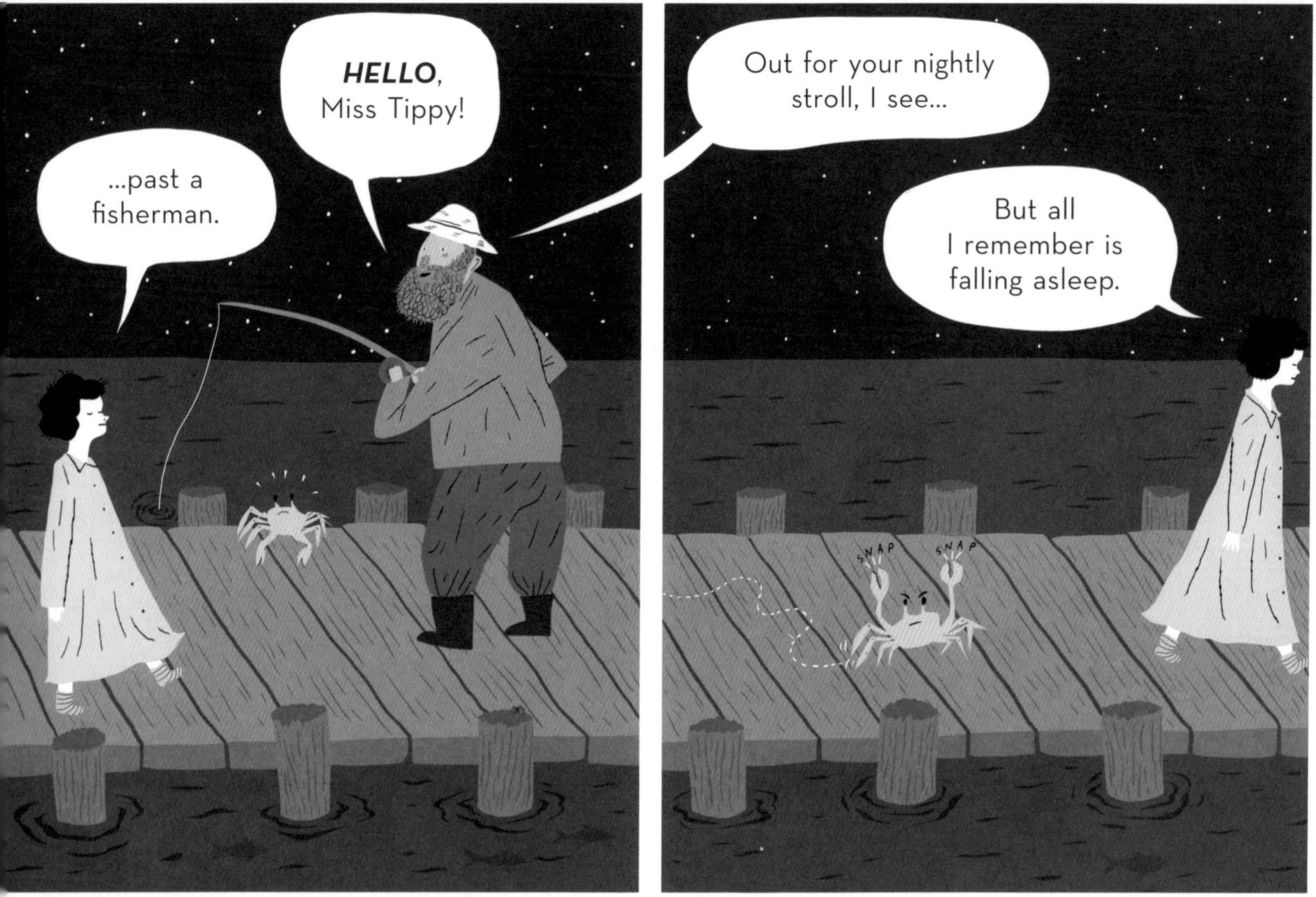
...past a fisherman.
HELLO, Miss Tippy!
Out for your nightly stroll, I see...
But all I remember is falling asleep.
SNAP
SNAP

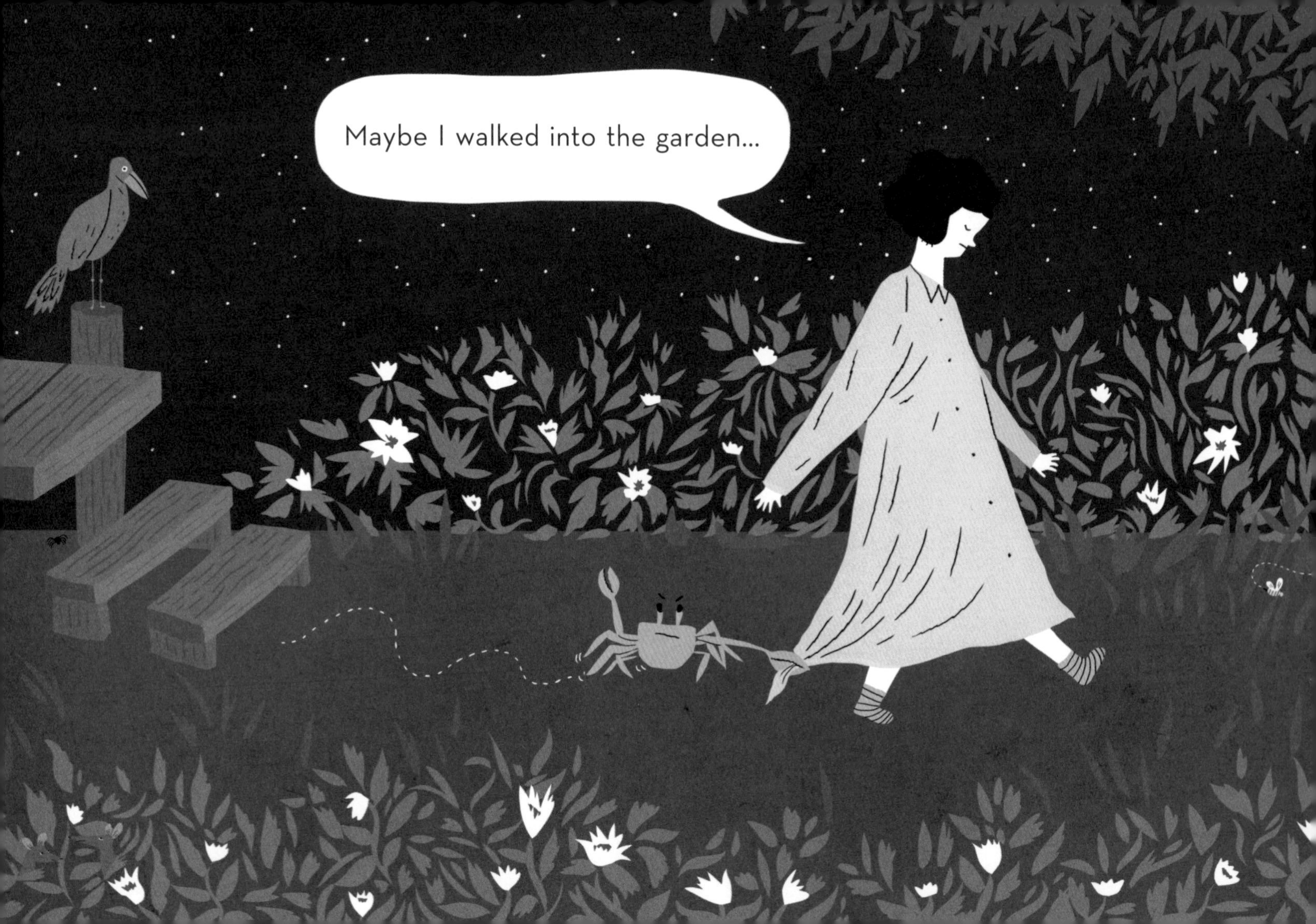
Maybe I walked into the garden...

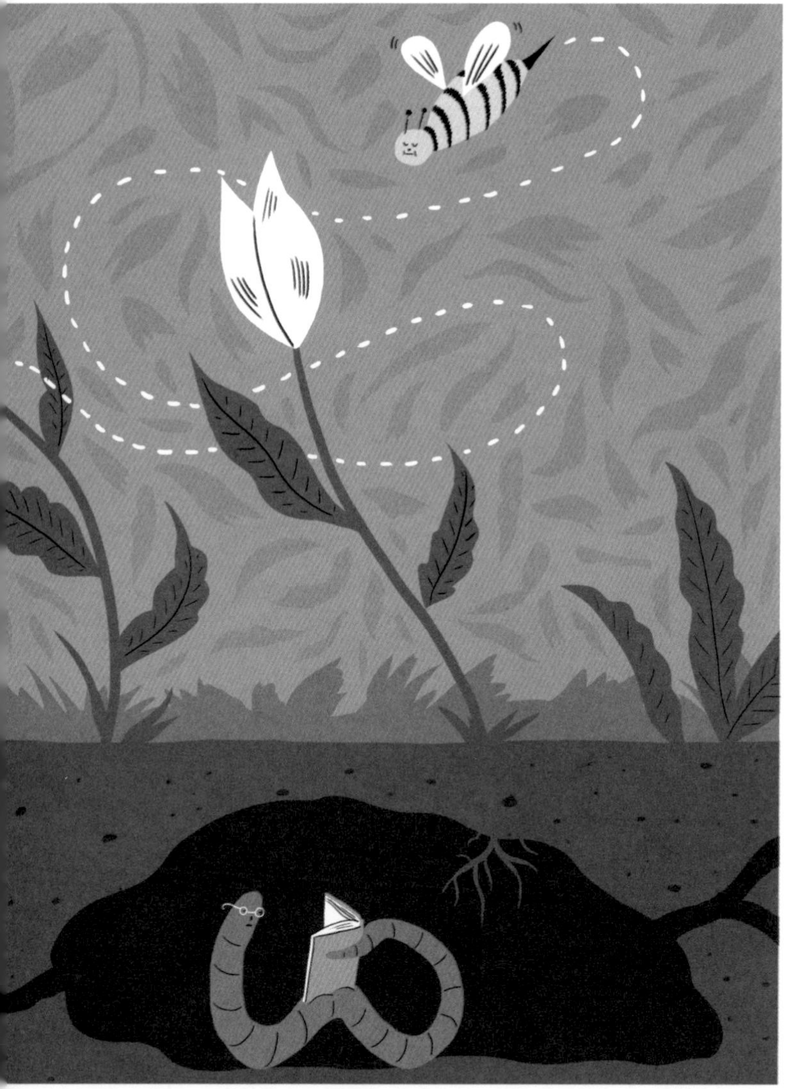

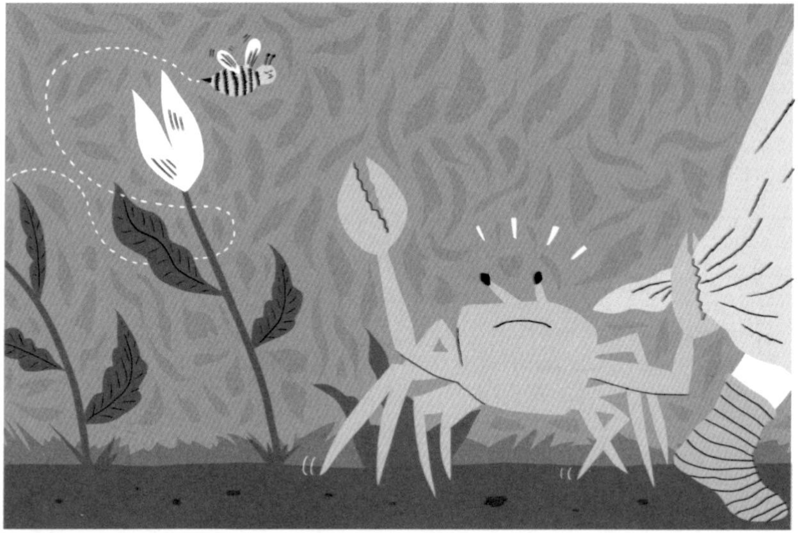

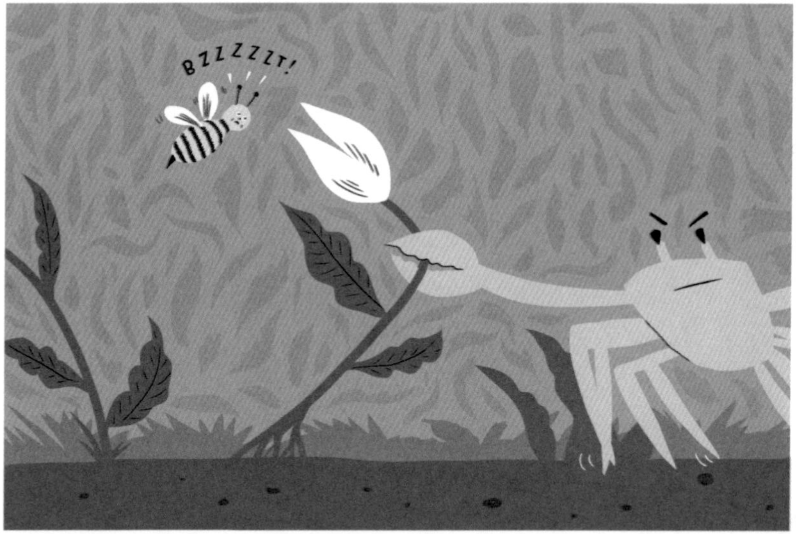
BZZZZZT!

...because I wanted to ***HOP*** across the lily pads...
...as the frogs croaked their night song.
CROAK
CROOAK
CROOAAK

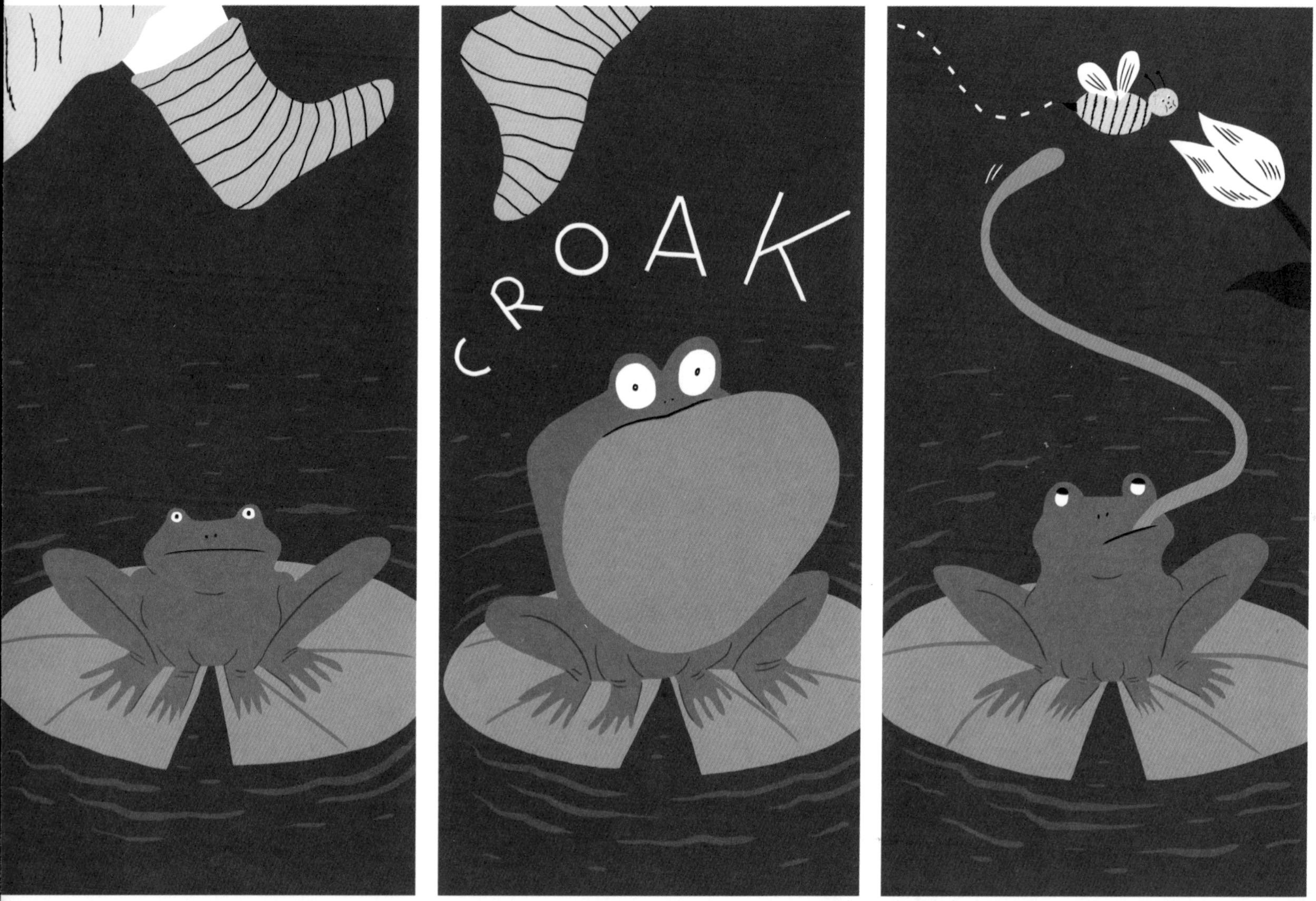
CROAK

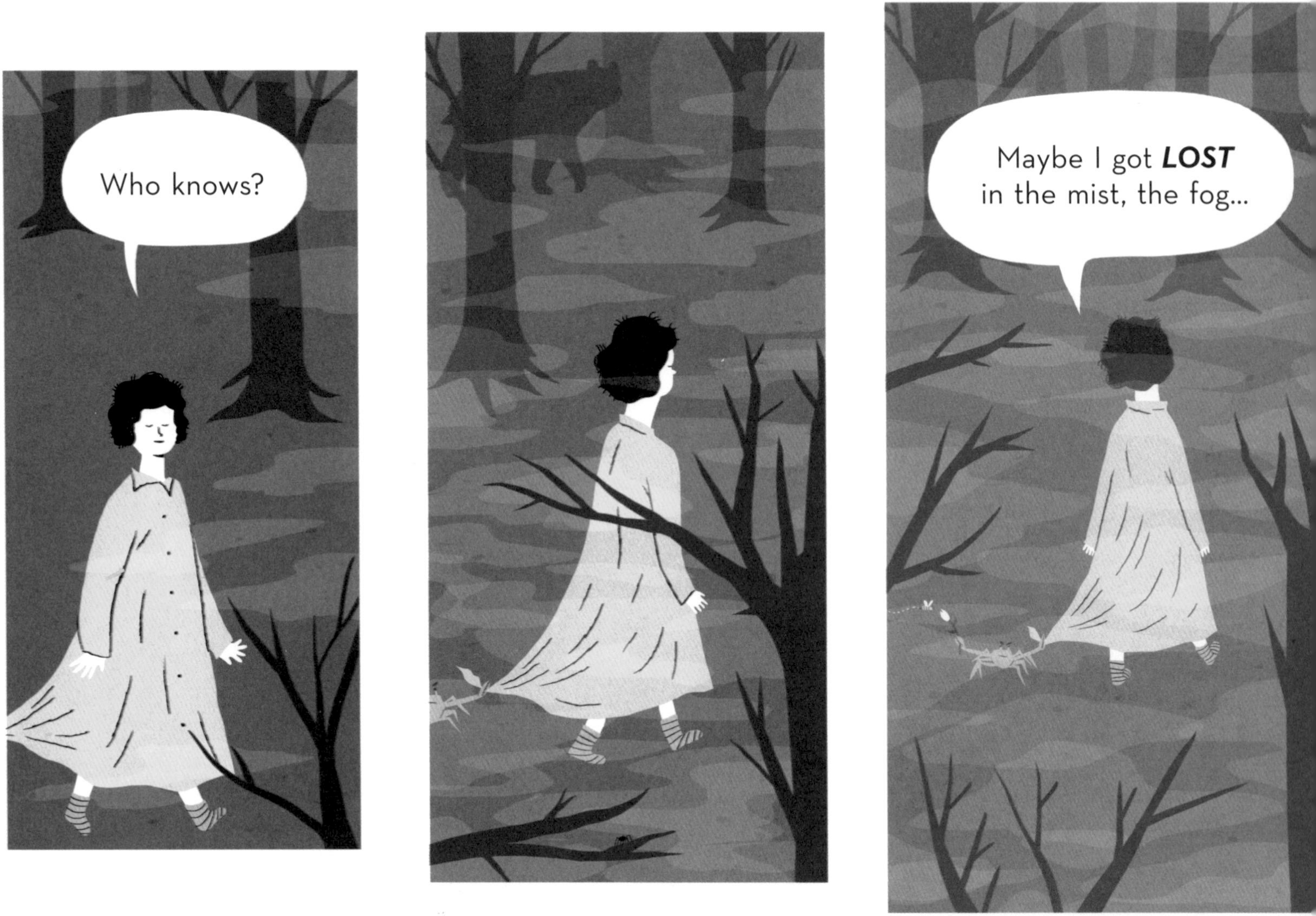
Who knows?
Maybe I got ***LOST***
in the mist, the fog...

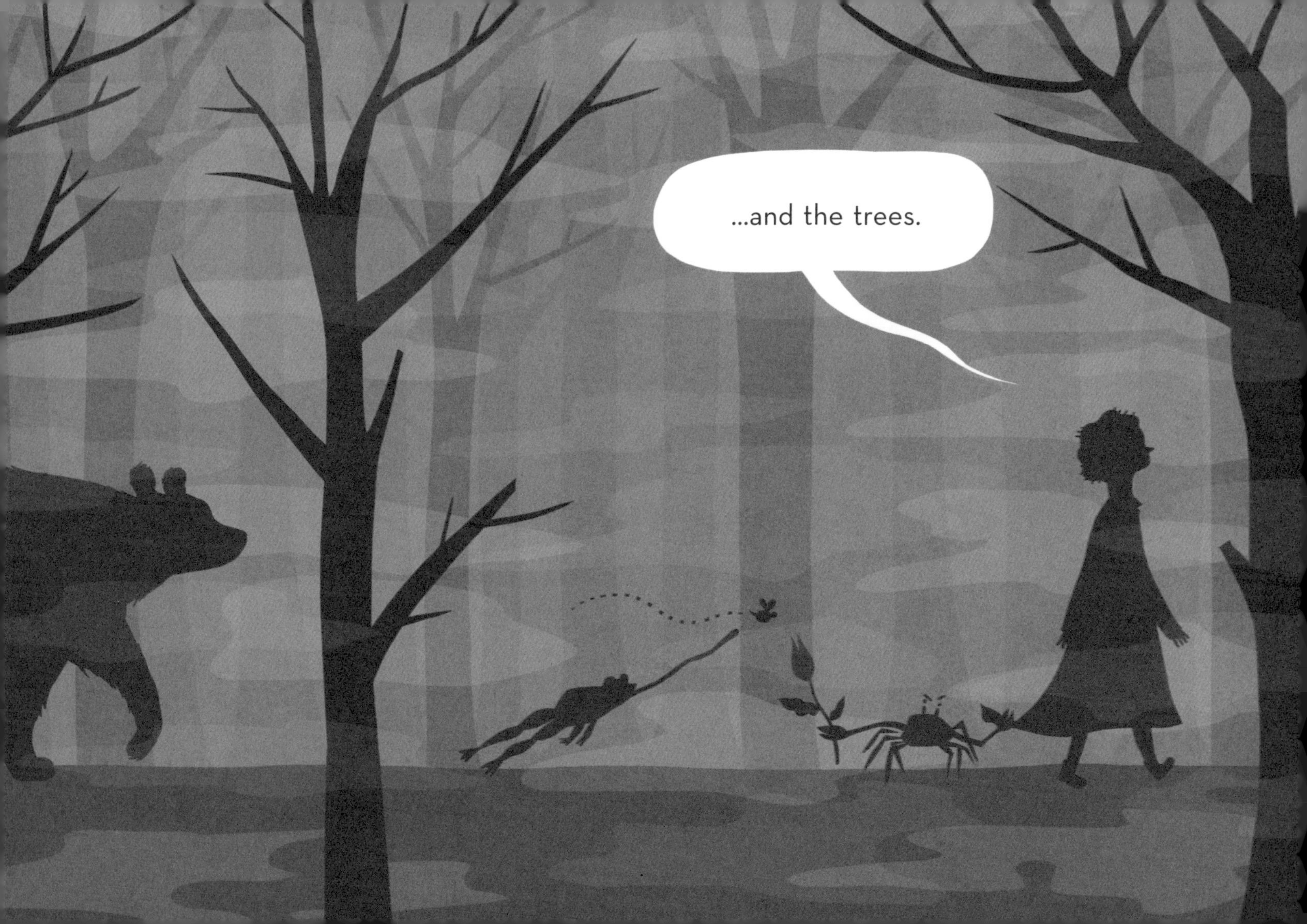
...and the trees.

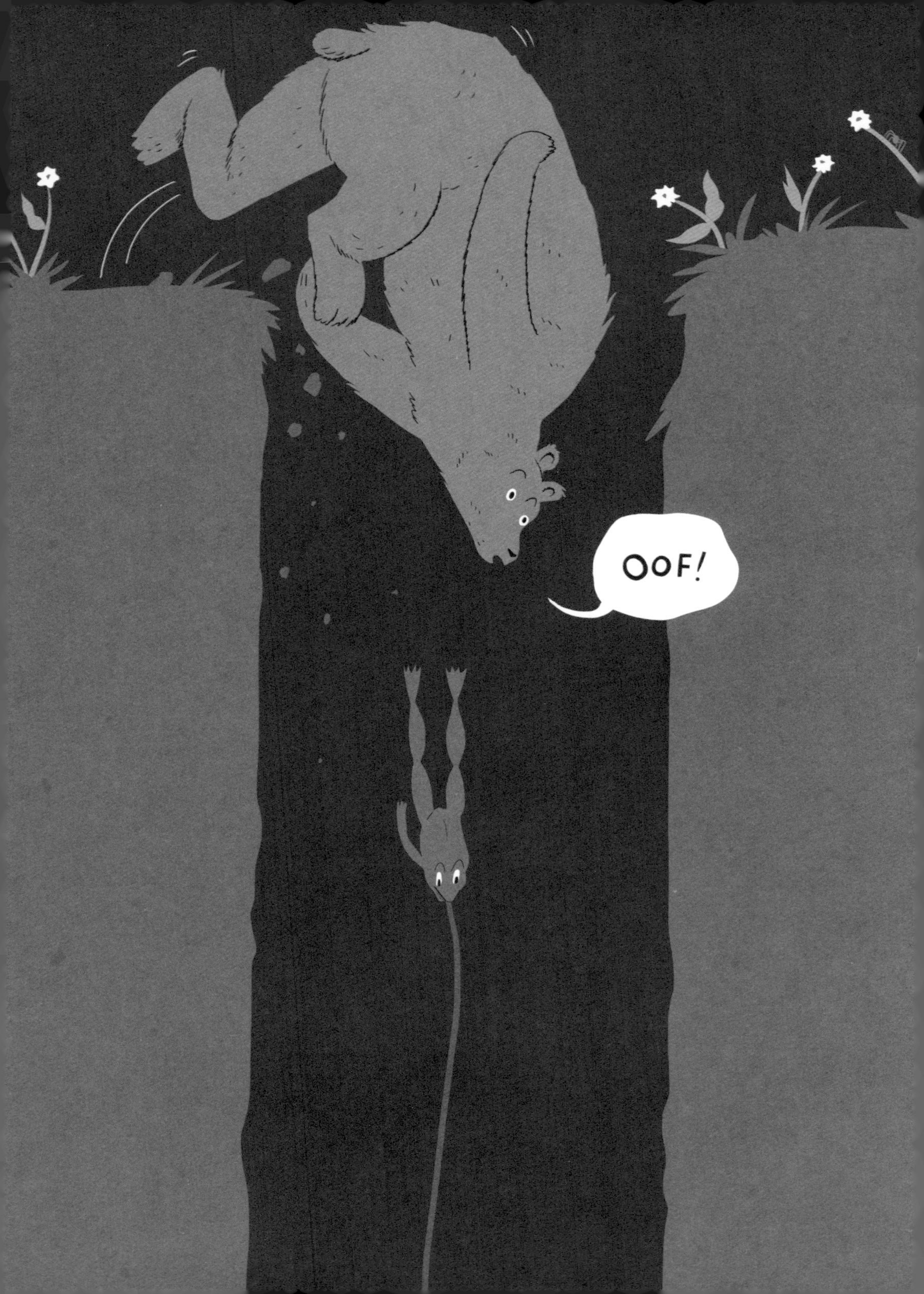
OOF!

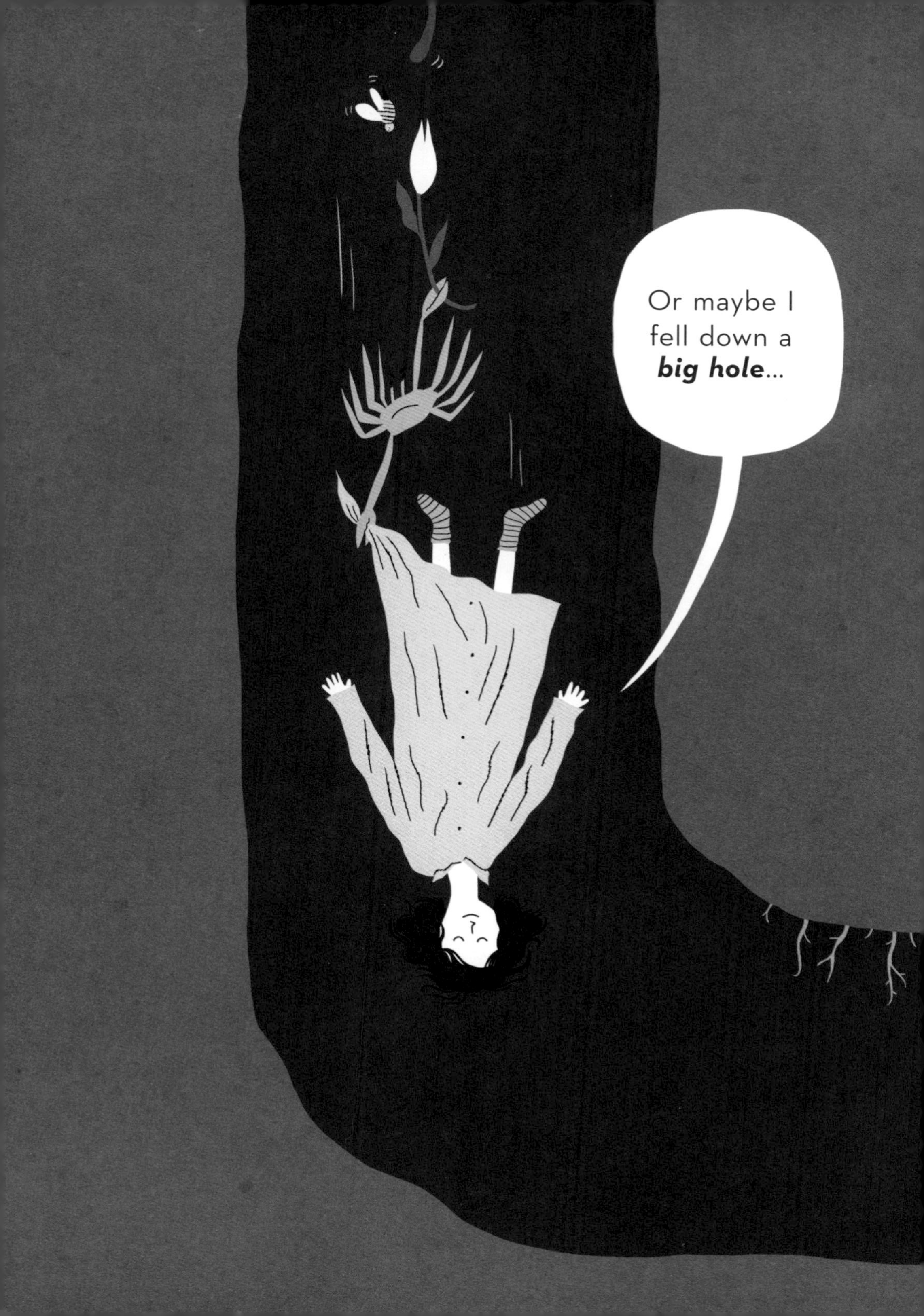
Or maybe I fell down a ***big hole***...

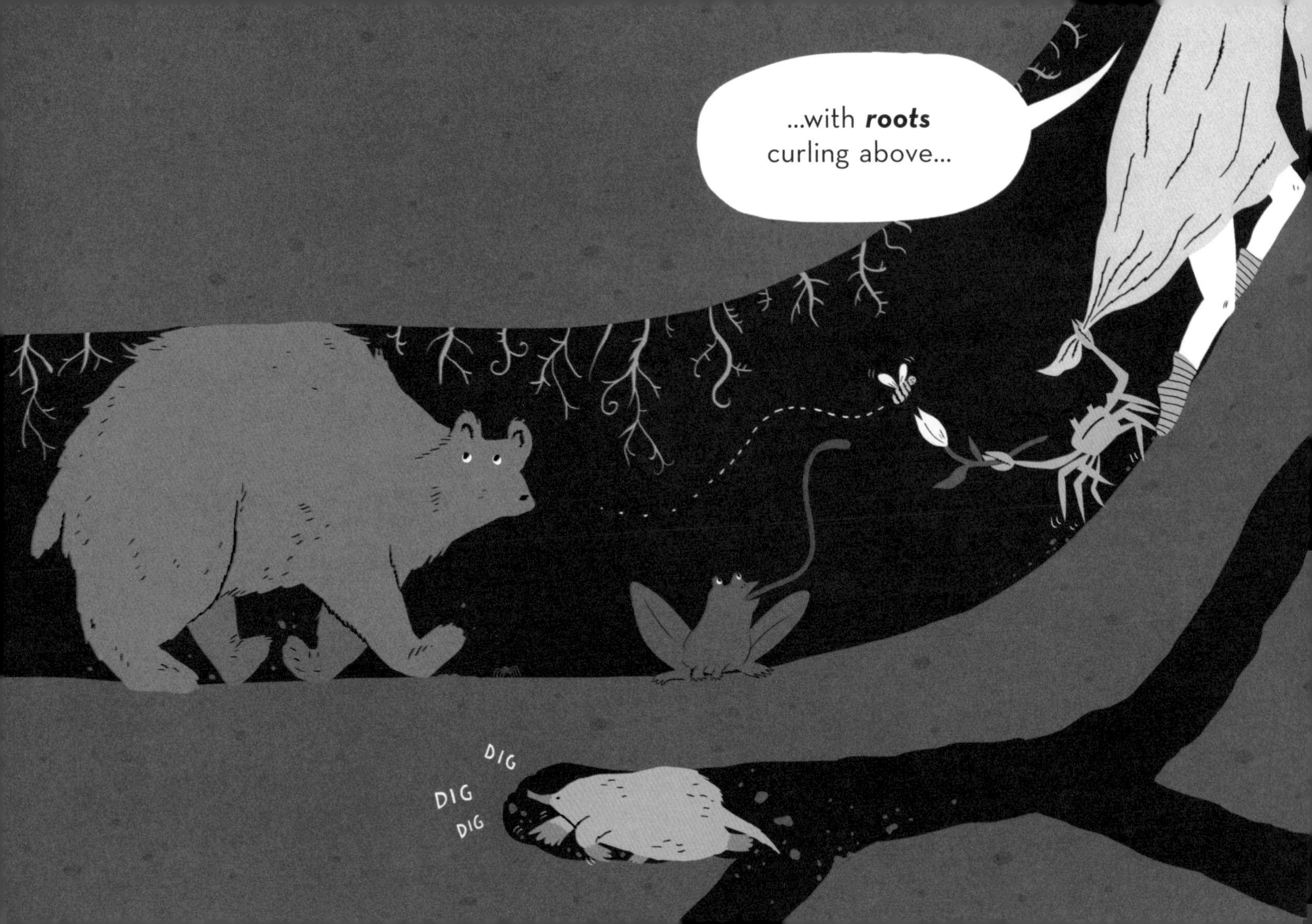
...with **roots** curling above...
DIG
DIG
DIG

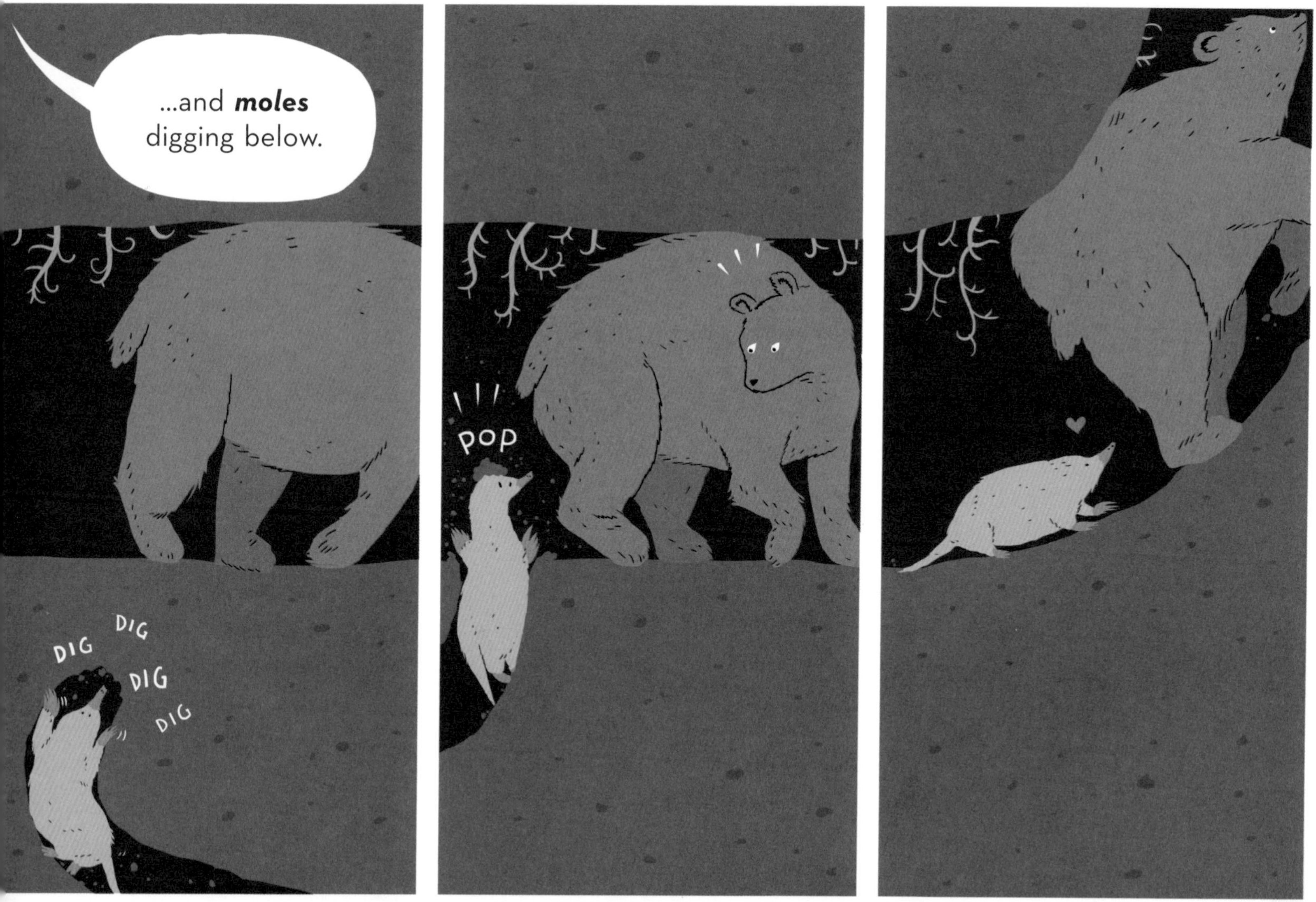

...and **moles** digging below.
DIG
DIG
DIG
DIG
POP

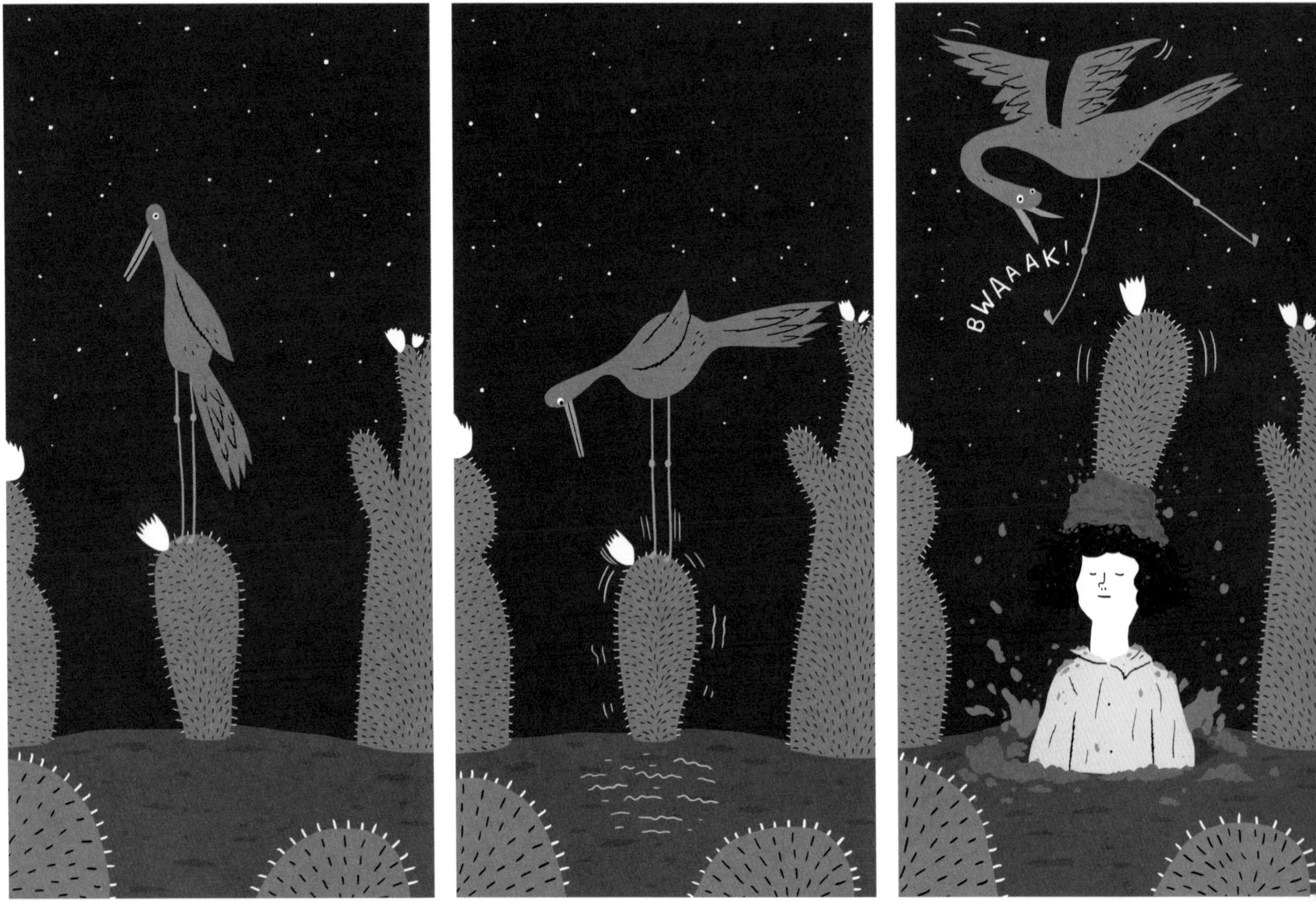
BWAAAK!

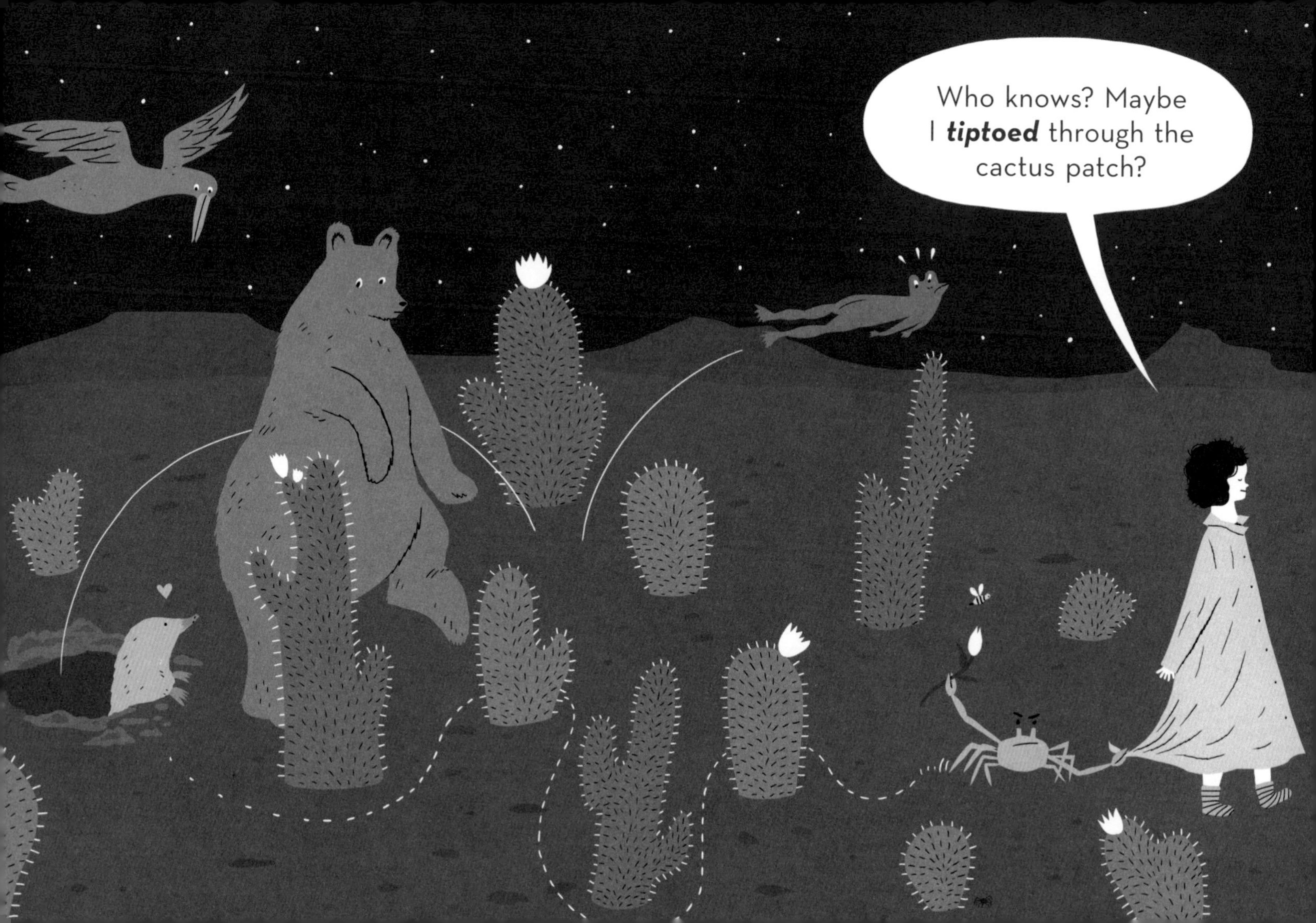
Who knows? Maybe I ***tiptoed*** through the cactus patch?

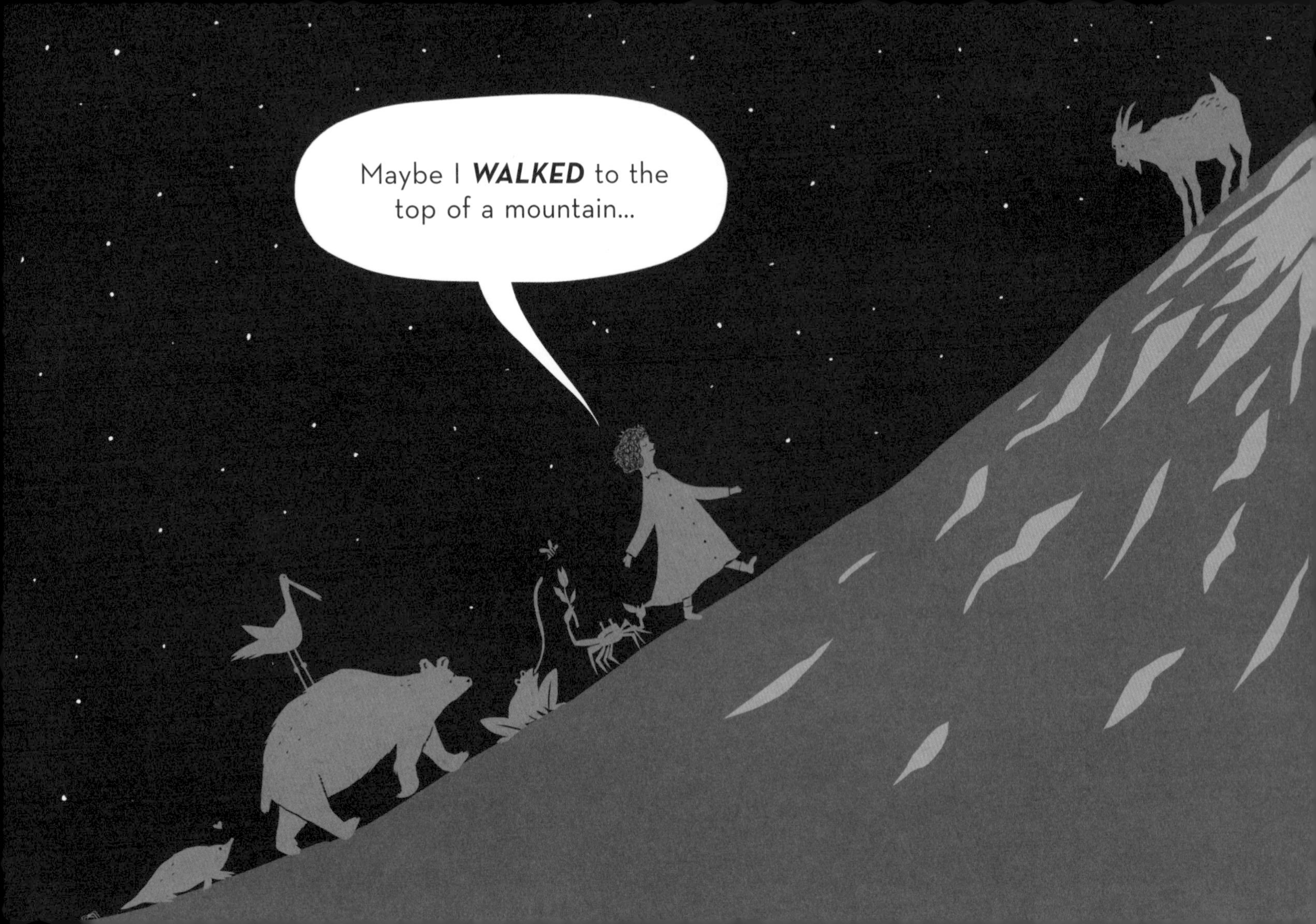
Maybe I **WALKED** to the top of a mountain...

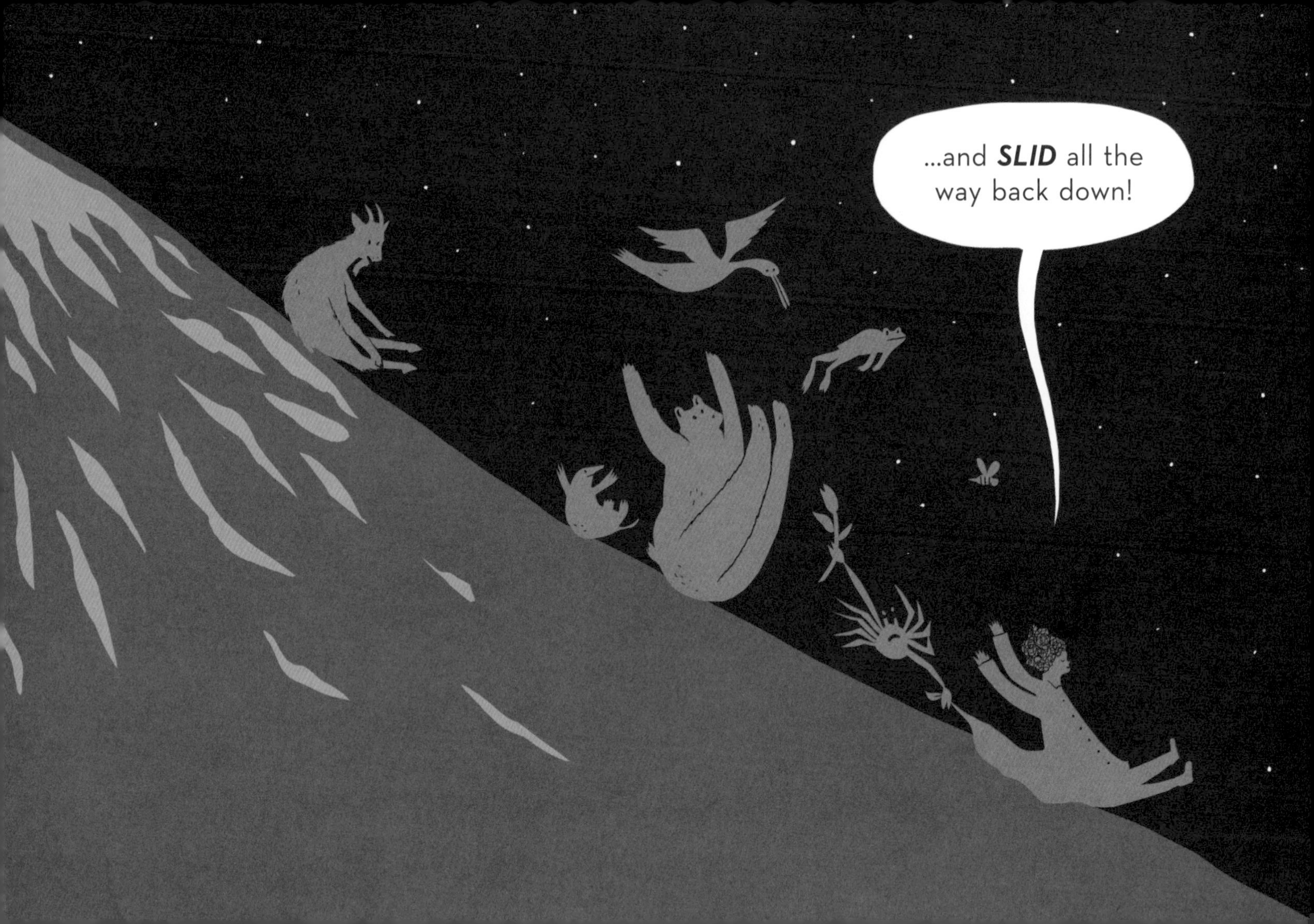
...and **SLID** all the way back down!

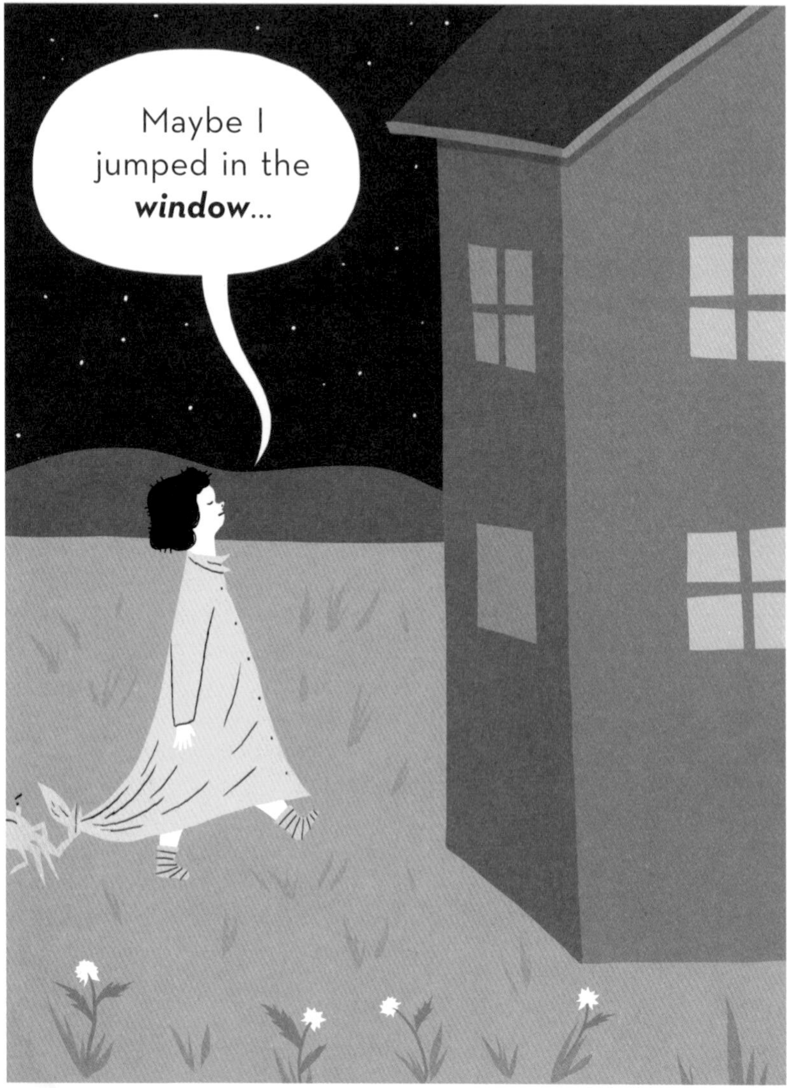
Maybe I jumped in the **window**...

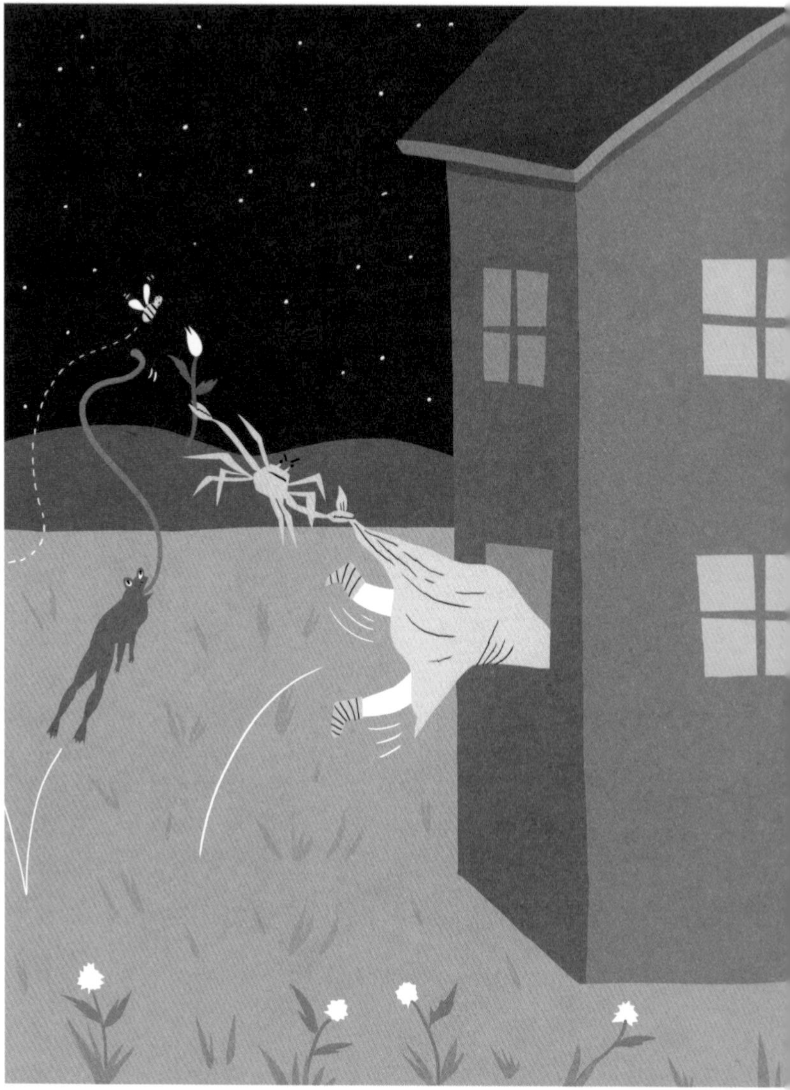

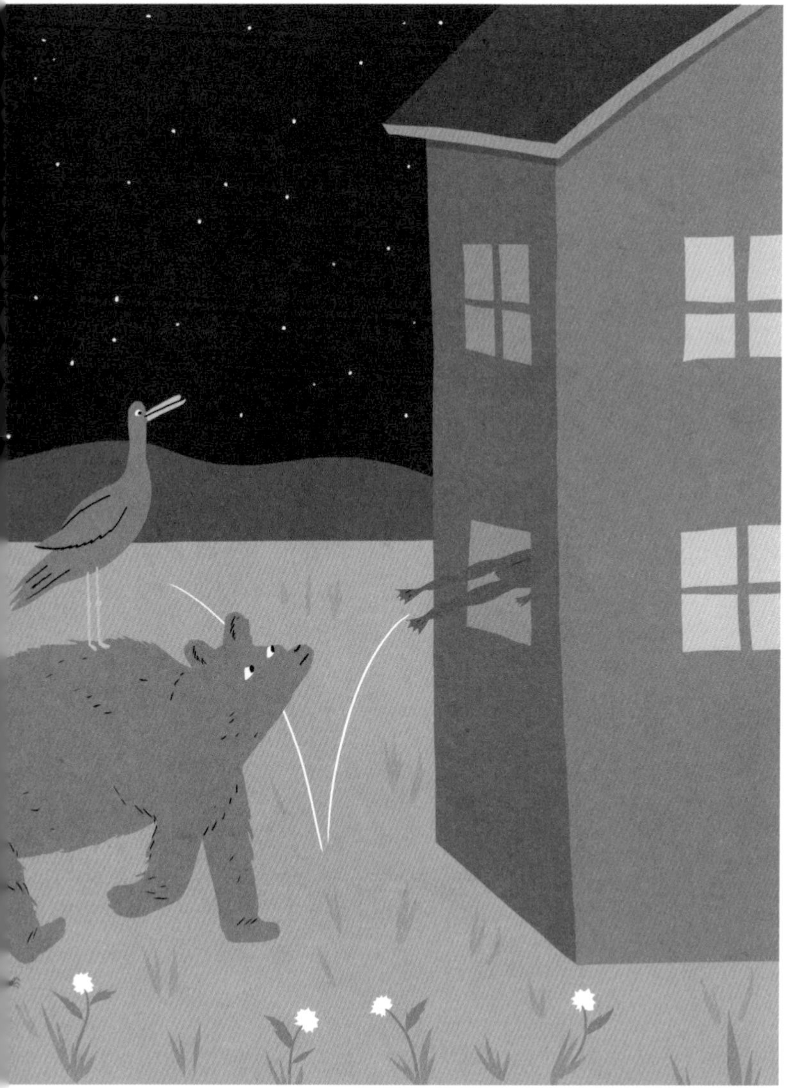

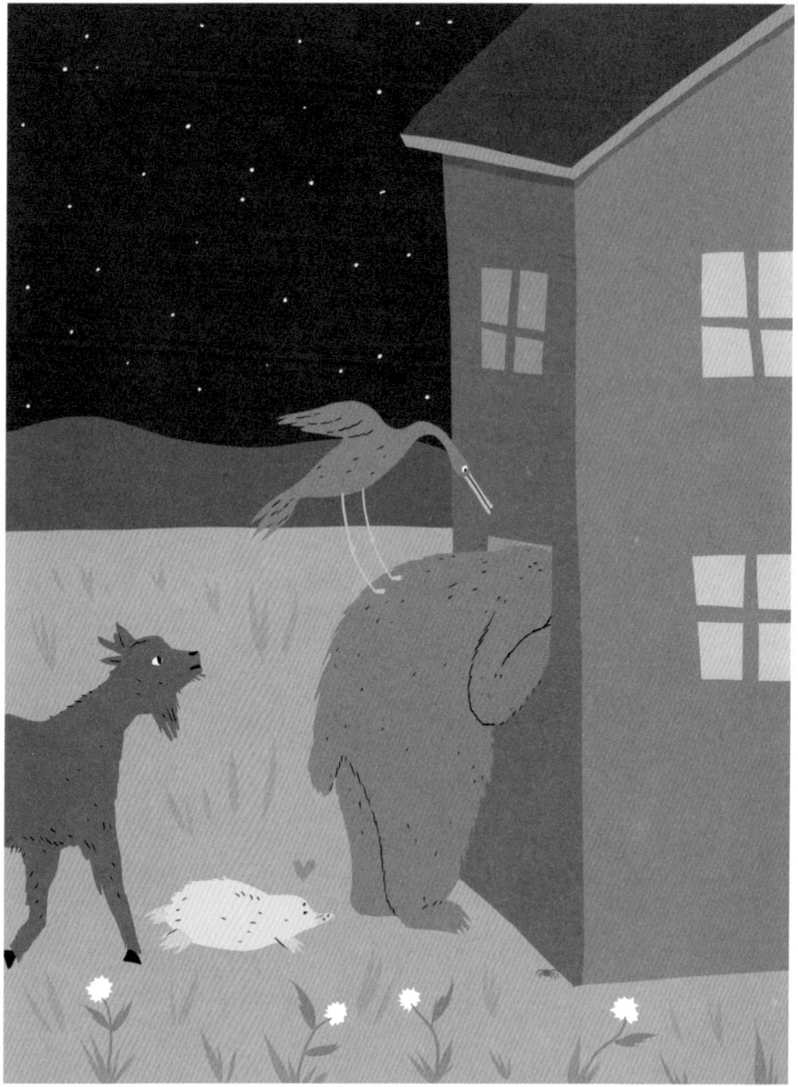

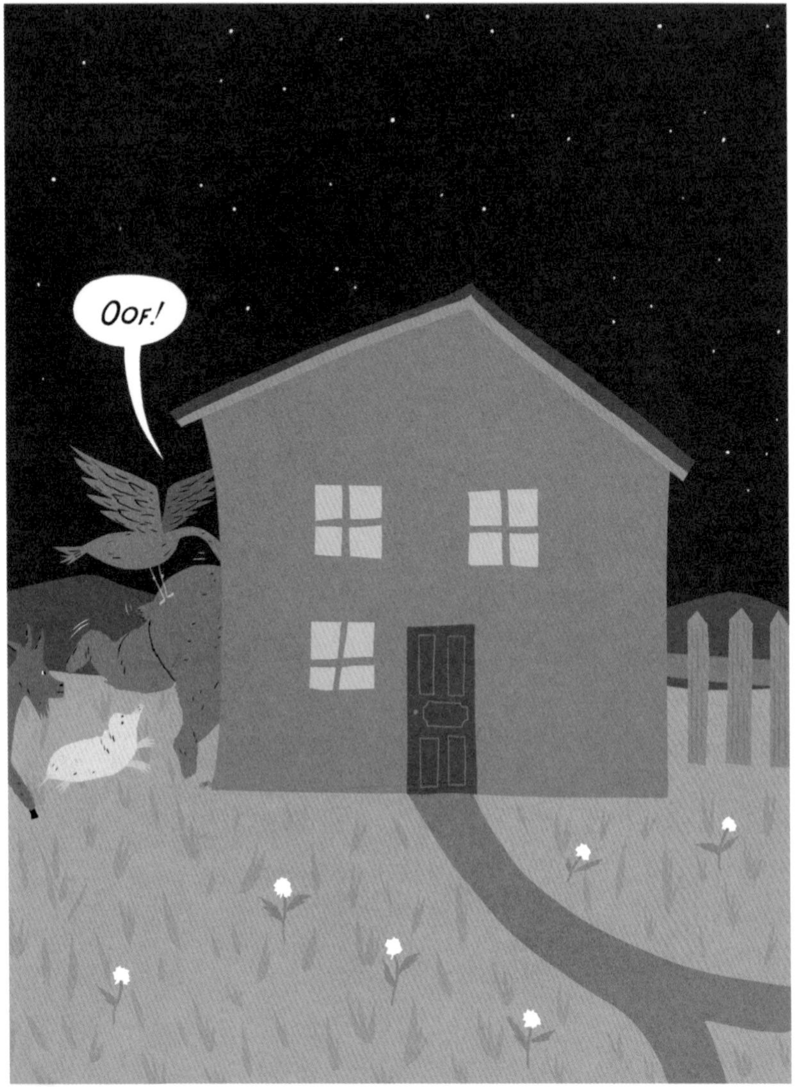
Oof!

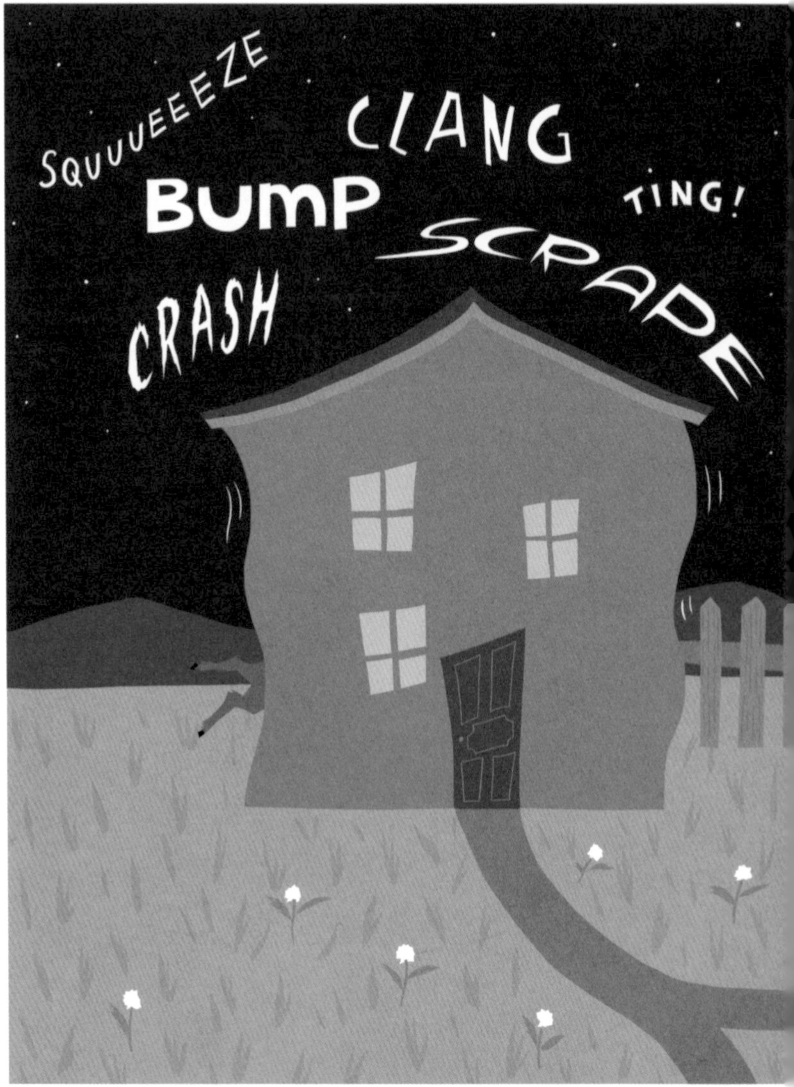
Squuueeeeze
Clang
Bump
Ting!
Scrape
Crash

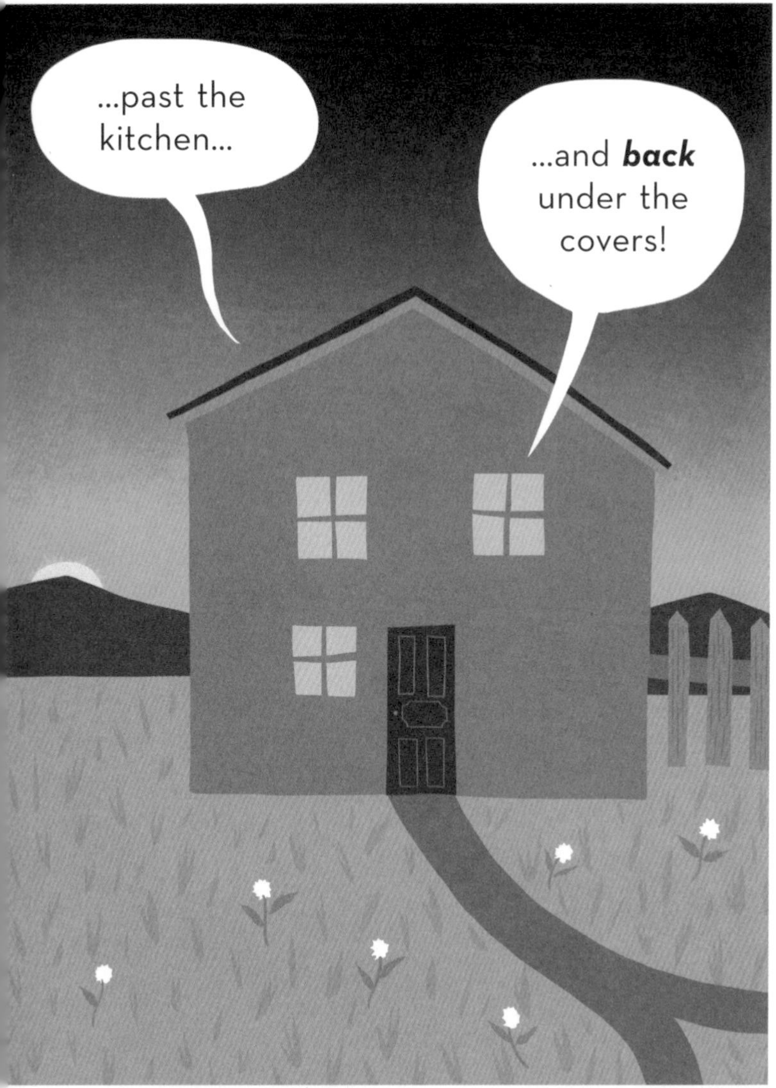
...past the kitchen...
...and **back** under the covers!

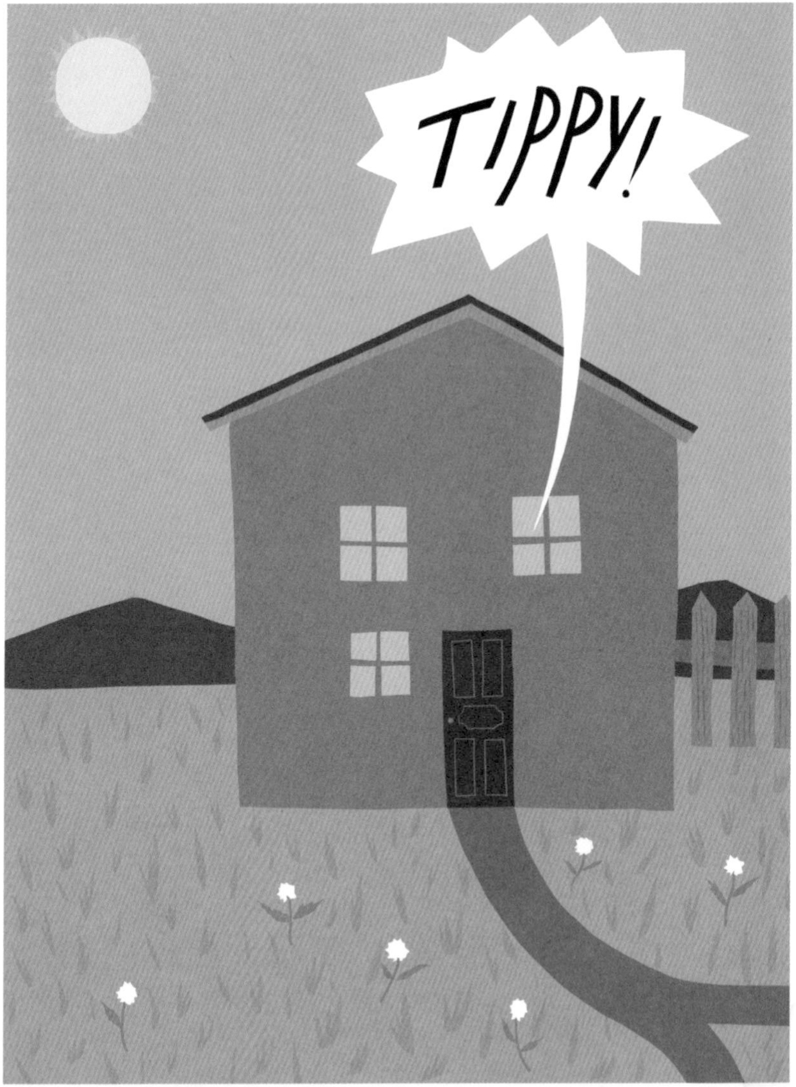
TIPPY!

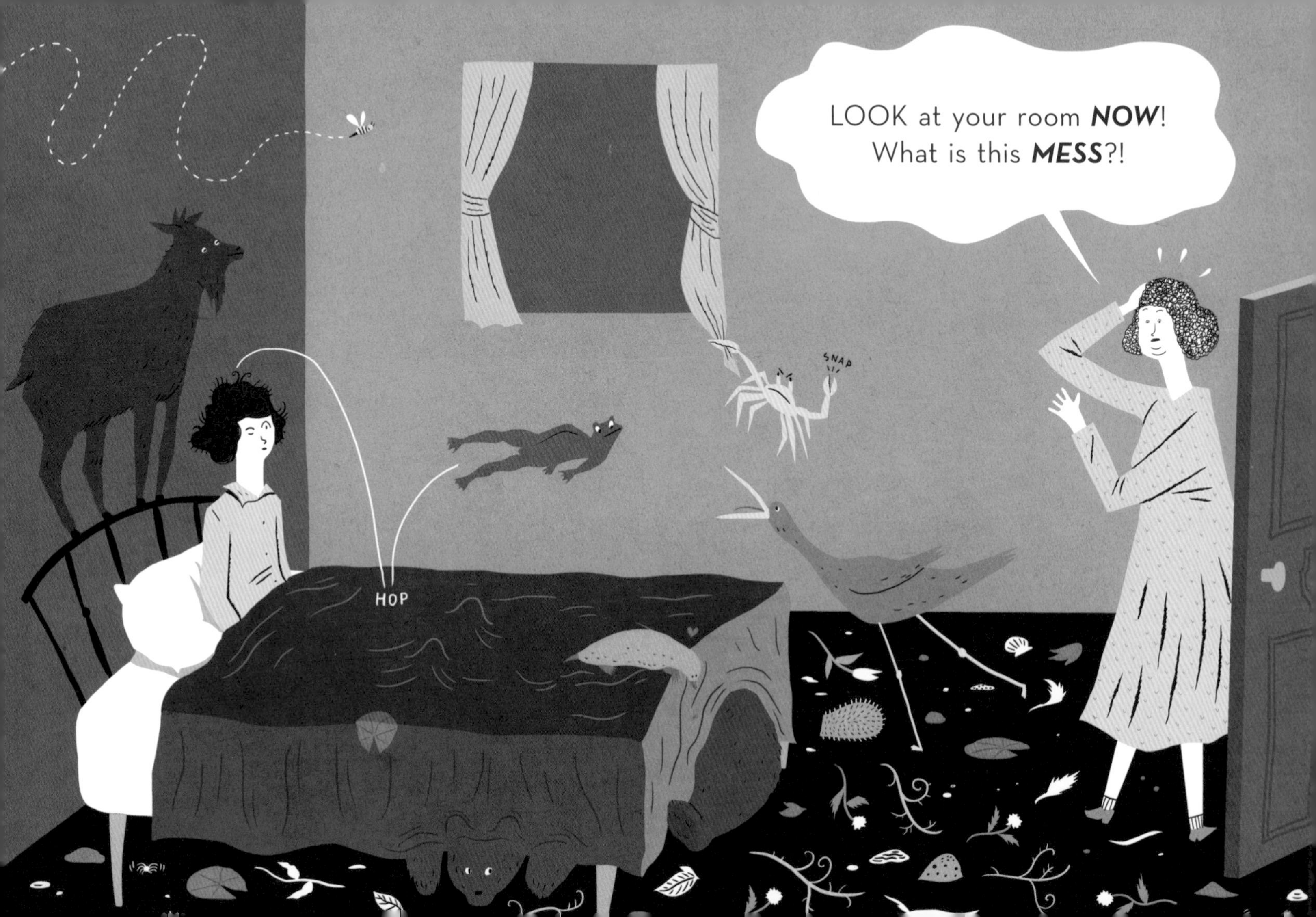
LOOK at your room **NOW**!
What is this **MESS**?!
SNAP
HOP

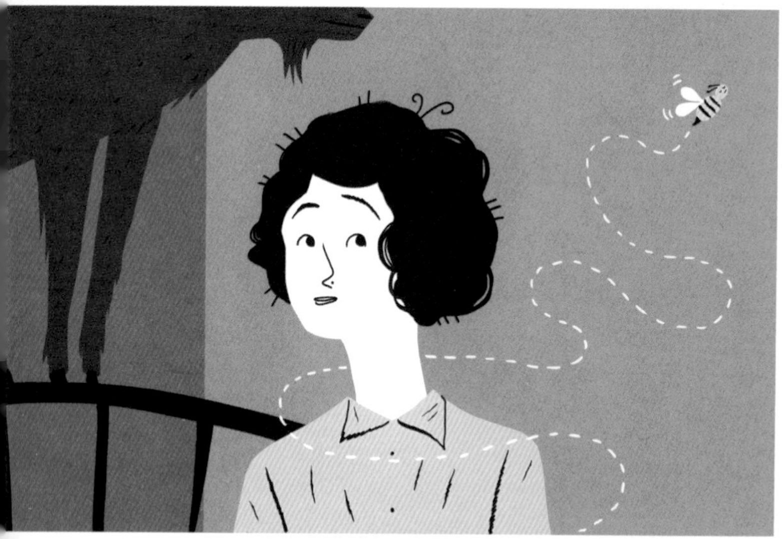

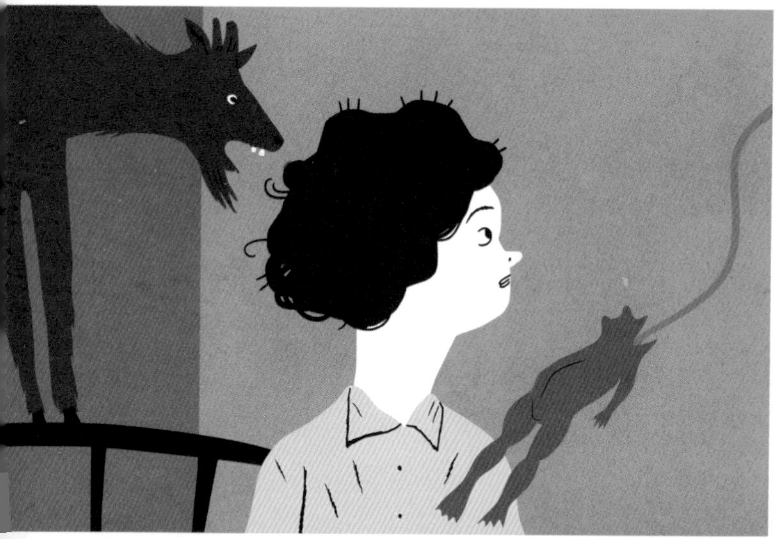

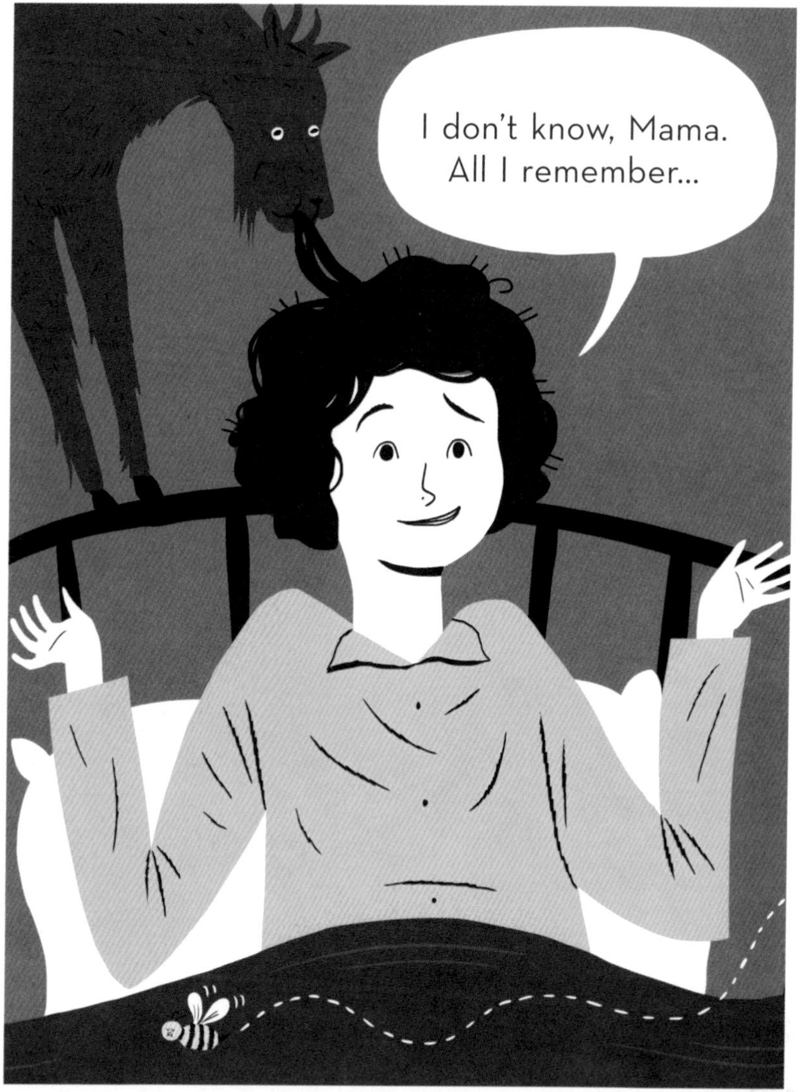
I don't know, Mama. All I remember...

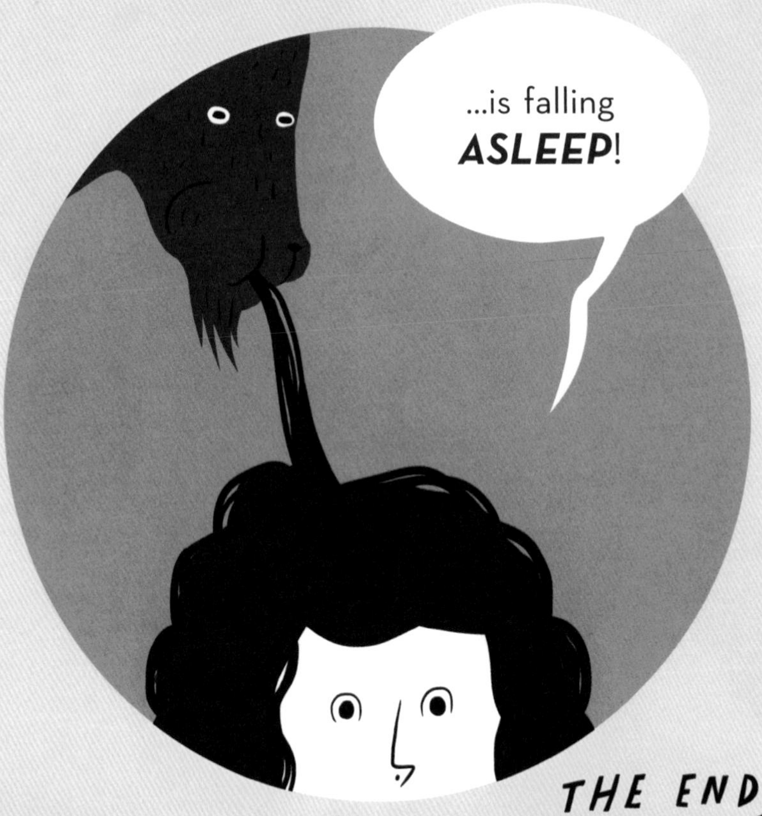
...is falling ASLEEP!

THE END

ABOUT THE AUTHOR

LILLI CARRÉ grew up in California and now lives in Chicago, Illinois, where she works as an artist, a filmmaker, and an illustrator. This is her first book for children.

As a kid, Lilli always dreamed of having wild animals follow her, but it usually ended up the other way around. Now she likes to take long, wandering walks around the city. No one has ever told her that she sleepwalks, but she often wakes up to find herself in a very messy room, occasionally with a cat on her head.

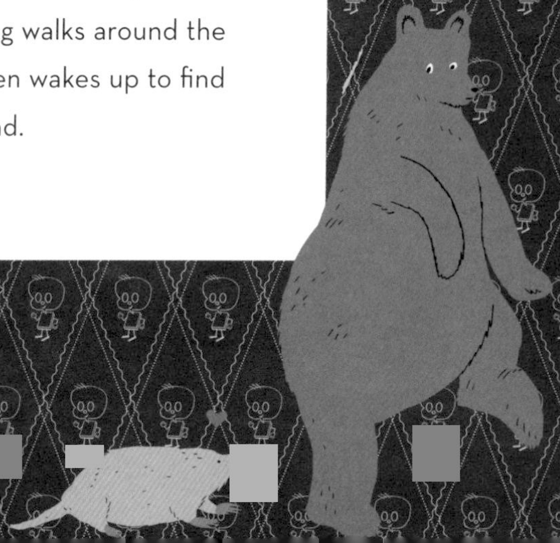

HOW TO READ COMICS WITH KIDS

Kids love comics! They are naturally drawn to the details in the pictures, which make them want to read the words. Comics beg for repeated readings and let both emerging and reluctant readers enjoy complex stories with a rich vocabulary. But since comics have their own grammar, here are a few tips for reading them with kids:

GUIDE YOUNG READERS: Use your finger to show your place in the text, but keep it at the bottom of the speaking character so it doesn't hide the very important facial expressions.

HAM IT UP! Think of the comic book story as a play and don't hesitate to read with expression and intonation. Assign parts or get kids to supply the sound effects, a great way to reinforce phonics skills.

LET THEM GUESS. Comics provide lots of context for the words, so emerging readers can make informed guesses. Like jigsaw puzzles, comics ask readers to make connections, so check a young audience's understanding by asking "What's this character thinking?" (but don't be surprised if a kid finds some of the comics' subtle details faster than you).

TALK ABOUT THE PICTURES. Point out how the artist paces the story with pauses (silent panels) or speeded-up action (a burst of short panels). Discuss how the size and shape of the panels carry meaning.

ABOVE ALL, ENJOY! There is of course never one right way to read, so go for the shared pleasure. Once children make the story happen in their imagination, they have discovered the thrill of reading, and you won't be able to stop them. At that point, just go get them more books, and more comics.

www.TOON-BOOKS.com

SEE OUR FREE ONLINE CARTOON MAKERS, LESSON PLANS, AND MUCH MORE

SNAP SNAP